Exe Post Facto

Lockwood and Darrow
Book 5

Suzy Bussell

Exe Post Facto

Lockwood and Darrow Book 5

By Suzy Bussell

Chapter One

Angus Darrow and Charlotte Lockwood, Devon private detectives, stood in the visitors' waiting area of Exeter Prison. They'd just passed through the airport-style security, had their bags X-rayed and walked through the metal-detector frame. Now they waited with the other visitors. There were twenty or so of them, all waiting to go through and meet their loved ones.

The waiting room was white and sterile, except for two rows of five plastic chairs bolted to the floor. The room was lit by a strip light because the small window had frosted glass.

Among the people were a middle-aged woman sat anxiously in a chair, her hands fidgeting in her lap. A young man, in a hoodie and tattoos, stood by the window, engrossed in his smartphone. An elderly couple held hands tightly in adjacent seats.

Charlotte shivered: her hackles were up. She didn't like being in a prison and had worn blue jeans and a black tunic top that went down to her knees. She moved closer to

Angus and whispered in his ear, "How long do you think we'll be waiting?"

Angus looked at his watch from underneath his crisp white shirt sleeve. "Not long. They're usually pretty efficient at getting everyone into the visitors' room quickly."

"Is it like you see in TV shows? You know, a table with you sitting on one side and the prisoner on the other?"

He nodded. "Pretty much."

A door at the front of the room opened and a prison guard appeared. "You can come through now, ladies and gentlemen."

Angus put his hand on Charlotte's arm. "Let everyone else go first."

Each prisoner was sitting behind a table and to Charlotte's surprise weren't dressed in a prison uniform, but their own clothes: a mixture of grey or black joggers and T-shirts. Their complexions were pale from lack of exposure to the sun, and there was a mixture of ages and appearances. Some rugged and rough, others with buzz cut heads and lots of tattoos.

Each visitor greeted their prisoner, hugging over the table, then sat down.

Angus spotted their potential client in the middle of the room, looking at the doorway. He recognised him from the news reports a few months ago, a man in his mid-forties, with large brown eyes and a rugged look. "Liam Beckett?" he asked, as he approached the table.

Liam's face, which had been anxious, lit up. He stood up and Angus held out his hand. "Angus Darrow, and this is my colleague Charlotte."

Charlotte nodded to him and they all sat down. There was a general hubbub of noise in the background as Angus took out his notebook.

"Thank you for coming." Liam rubbed his hand over his face. "I didn't think you'd turn up."

Angus met his eyes. "I never break a promise."

"Angus is a man of his word," Charlotte gave Liam a reassuring smile.

Liam glanced at her, then nodded. "I'm sorry. It's just, well, I thought everyone had written me off. After my conviction a few months ago, the few friends I had disappeared. My daughter doesn't want to know, either. That's the hardest thing. Being stuck in here" – he glanced around briefly – "knowing everyone hates me and wants me dead."

He sighed. "I've thought about ending it all, you know? But I know I'm innocent, and if I die, the fact that I'm innocent dies with me." He gazed at them both. "You have to help me!"

Angus opened his notebook and took out his pen. "All right, let's start from the beginning. You want to hire us to prove your innocence of the murder you were convicted of a few months ago? Brian Letterman, your next-door neighbour."

"Yes."

Angus studied him. "I've met a lot of men who profess their innocence simply because they want to get away with their crime. Why should we believe you?"

"I don't have any proof. I was set up, and I can't prove it." Liam slumped forward, crossed his arms on the table and buried his head in them.

Charlotte and Angus looked at each other, then Charlotte put a hand on Liam's arm. "Why don't you just tell us everything. We're here because you want to prove your innocence, but we need to know that you are actually innocent."

Liam lifted his head and looked at her. "I'm sorry. I used

to believe in the justice system. I know about miscarriages of justice, and people being proved innocent years after they've been convicted, but I can't face years shut in here. If I'd done it, I'd put up with the punishment, but I didn't. It's not right that I should rot in here. I haven't done anything wrong!"

Angus had been writing notes, raised his pen. "I've read the judge's summing-up in your case, and all the evidence points to you. What makes you think we can find evidence that the police didn't?"

"I don't know. All I do know is that someone made it look as if I did it. I have to at least try to clear my name." He faced them, defiant. "I've got money, if that's what you're worried about. When that's gone, I can sell my house. I don't care if I have nothing, as long as I get out of here."

Charlotte turned to Angus. He decided which cases they took on, and his expression was as cool as usual. Practiced and perfected by his time as police detective.

Angus put his pen on the table. "Why don't you tell us more about the case."

"Me and Brian didn't get on. We live – lived next door to each other, in two semi-detached farm workers' cottages. I was there first: I moved in four years ago. He moved in a few months later."

"You owned the properties?"

"I owned mine. Bought it outright, but Brian rented from the landowner. At first we got on, but things went haywire when he removed a bush from my garden because it overhung his hedge. I went ballistic at him. Daft, maybe, but it was on my land and he had no right. From then on, it was basically all-out war."

"What happened next?"

"We'd do things to wind each other up. I played loud

music just to annoy him. I even put weedkiller on his plants out front. It seems stupid now, sat here."

Charlotte glanced at Angus. It was stupid. Angus's face was still impassive, though. "And this continued right up until he died?" he asked.

Liam nodded. "But I didn't kill him. I swear it."

"Tell me about the day he was murdered."

Liam sat back and sighed. "I've gone over this a million times already with the police." He stared at Angus, who didn't flinch, then sighed again. "I came back from work and put my music on loud. Brian banged on the wall to tell me to shut up, but I ignored him. I made myself dinner and after I'd eaten I went out into the garden and there was dog poo on my lawn. He'd done that before: thrown it over to annoy me. He didn't even have a dog. So I went round to his house and banged on the front door. He opened it and we had a screaming row. Called each other every name under the sun." He shrugged. "I said I was going to smear dog poo over his stupid face."

"You didn't threaten to kill him?"

"No. And I didn't kill him. I felt like it, but I never even hit him. I pushed him, sure, but he hit *me*."

"How did the confrontation end?"

"With that. He landed a lucky punch on me and got me in the face. I could feel blood coming out of my nose, so I went back to mine to sort myself out. Stupid thing was, he said he never threw the dog poo on my lawn. He kept denying he'd done it. But who else would it be?"

"You said someone set you up. Maybe it was that person..." Angus asked.

Liam's eyes widened. "Yeah, I've thought about that. But Brian was vindictive. It wasn't unlike him at all."

"Did you ever think about setting up a CCTV camera?" Charlotte asked.

Liam shook his head. "I should have done. Wish I had. Then I could have proved I never left my house after that argument."

"And you didn't go anywhere that night? Not even to the shop or supermarket?" Angus asked.

"No. I went back in to cool off. But first I picked up the dog poo with a hoe and threw it over the hedge into his garden."

"And the police arrested you the next day?"

"Yeah. It was in the evening. I got back from work and there was a police car parked up outside the house. They arrested me not long after."

There was a long silence as Angus and Charlotte mulled this over. "Is there anything else you can tell me about the night of the argument?" asked Angus. "Did you see anyone else go into Brian's house?"

Liam shook his head. "It was almost dark when we argued. I shut the curtains when I got back in, then watched telly. I wanted to shut him out, forget about it."

Angus finished the sentence he was writing and looked up. "All right, we'll start an investigation and look into this. I won't string you along, Liam. We'll do our best, but if we hit a dead end, we'll stop. And if I find anything that further confirms your guilt, I won't hide that, either."

Liam's face flooded with relief. "You won't find anything like that because I didn't do it. I'll make sure my lawyers give you everything you need. I'll phone them as soon as I'm allowed. And if you need to ask me any questions, anything at all, just ask. To be honest, though, it's all in the police reports and the courtroom transcripts. I've been over and over it."

Angus nodded. "I'll keep you up to date. We'll start as soon as you've signed the papers and got your lawyers to pay our deposit."

A sort of half sob, half hiccup burst out of Liam. "You don't know what this means to me. I can't thank you enough."

Angus allowed himself a smile. "We're not making any promises, but we'll do our best." He put his notepad and pen away and stood up, Charlotte and Liam followed suit. Angus held out his hand again to Liam. "I'll be in touch."

Outside the prison Charlotte turned to Angus. "I've never met a convicted killer before.""He could be innocent."

"I know, but he *is* a convicted killer. A guilty convicted killer is something else..." Charlotte halted and looked at Angus. "If we're taking the case, surely we need to believe that Liam is actually innocent?"

Angus shrugged. "We've been hired to prove his innocence, but we need to keep an open mind and look at everything objectively. Assume nothing."

"That sounds like a good approach. He certainly seemed to believe he was innocent." Charlotte said. "I mean, he was emotional about it."

Angus nodded. "It was some good acting if he did do it."

"What will we do now? I mean, before he signs on the dotted line."

"I'll look at some more properties to invest in."

Charlotte considered this. "Interesting. Anything that's caught your eye so far?"

"A few."

"Well, if you need a second opinion, let me know. I love snooping around other people's houses. I watch all those property programmes where they buy a wreck and do it up, then sell it for a large profit." She looked puzzled. "Although the cost of the renovation always seems really cheap to me. Whenever I've had quotes from tradesmen, they're extortionate."

Angus smiled. "That's probably because they realise you're loaded and you can afford to pay more than most." He watched Charlotte's expression change as the penny dropped. She got in the car without another word.

Chapter Two

Back at his house in a housing estate in the north of Exeter, Angus picked up a few sheets of paper, held together by a clip. "This is Liam's original statement, and it's the same in his first police interview. He says that he lost his temper and went round to Brian's house. They argued outside, screaming and shouting at each other. He said they ended up pushing and shoving each other, but Brian was stronger than him and punched him, giving him a nosebleed."

"So far so good," said Charlotte. "He left, went home to stop the bleed, changed his clothes because there was blood all over them and calmed down. He said he didn't leave the house after that. The following evening, the police called round and arrested him for Brian's murder."

Angus picked up another report. "This is the transcript of his second interview with the police, a day later. His account of what happened is the same: it doesn't deviate at all from the first."

Then he picked up a small pile of sheets. "This is the

trial transcript. It's longer, especially the part where he was cross-examined by the prosecution, but it's the same."

"So he's consistent," Charlotte stated. "Which means...?"

"Have you ever heard the saying 'It's better to tell the truth because it's easier to remember'?" Angus asked her.

Charlotte raised her eyebrows. "Is that why you never lie?"

"It's one of the reasons..." Angus mused. "But I can't help thinking that he's telling the truth because he's never swayed from what he originally said. Each time he's asked, he gives the same account. It's common for criminals to add things or miss things out when they're trying to cover up their crimes."

"And he hasn't done that, so you think he's innocent."

"Yes, basically. Even when he gave an account of it again earlier, it was the same." Angus sat down and ran his hands through his hair. "I trust my gut feelings about people too, and when we met him, I got the impression that he was telling the truth. I just don't know how we'll prove it."

"Start at the beginning?"

"Yes. I want to talk to the investigating officer first. Then we need to look into the victim and find out if there was even a hint of anyone else who might want him dead."

"Who was the chief investigating officer? It wasn't my brother, was it?" Charlotte laughed at her own joke.

Angus stared at Charlotte. "It was Woody, yes."

Charlotte's eyes widened. "You're not joking. Why didn't you tell me before now?" She gasped. "Shit! He may be my brother, but he'll kill me when he realises we're investigating a conviction that *he* brought." Charlotte put her head in her hands.

After a moment, Angus came to sit next to Charlotte

and put his arm around her. She instantly stilled. "I did know that Woody was the chief investigating officer, but I also knew that if you found out before we saw Liam, you'd have nothing to do with it. Charlotte, we're being hired by a man who claims he is innocent. The Crown Prosecution Service looked at the evidence and decided whether or not to take the case to court, not your brother. The fact that a jury convicted Liam means that he might well be guilty."

Charlotte looked up at Angus, their faces inches apart. Angus felt her body relax. "Wait. Does Liam know I'm Mark's sister? I'm sure he wouldn't want to hire me if he knew I was related to the man who helped put him in prison."

Angus took a deep breath. "Liam doesn't know you're Mark's sister. Anyway, officially he's hiring me, not you."

"But won't he want to know my background if I'm working on this case with you?"

Angus shrugged. "I introduced you as Charlotte: I didn't use your surname for a reason. Liam doesn't know you're Woody's sister, and there's no reason why he should. You're not officially part of the business, remember. Our arrangement is informal. Anyway, I understand you well enough by now to know that you'll investigate with an open mind."

"Of course I will." Charlotte leaned back into Angus's chest and Angus tried to calm his racing heart. "I'll do everything I can to make sure I get to the truth, even if it means making it public that my brother got it wrong. But it's still going to make things incredibly difficult for me. Mark and Fiona were my rock when my marriage broke up. He'll hate me."

Angus considered how to phrase his next words. "I don't think he'll take it personally, Charlotte. He'll be annoyed at first, no doubt, because everyone has their pride, but I've been thinking about this. If I was in his place and I'd done everything I could to get to the truth of a case, then someone came along to dig it all back up, yes, I would be annoyed. Ultimately, though, if it turned out that I hadn't got to the truth, I'd put aside my pride."

Charlotte looked up at him. "That's because you're a good man."

"So is Woody."

"So who's going to tell him?"

"I will. I wouldn't leave it to you. It's my decision to take the case."

"Well, let me know when you're going to tell him and I'll check to make sure he hasn't murdered you." Angus felt her body move as she chuckled.

Chapter Three

A few days later, the deposit was paid and it was time to tell Woody. Angus sat outside Woody's house in his car for a few minutes, running through what he was going to say. It would either go very well, or very badly. He and Woody went back a long way. They worked on many cases together, and had come out of it not exactly close, but with a mutual respect that rarely persisted and endured outside the force. Angus considered it a friendship.

Since Angus had left the police, he'd had more contact with Woody than with any other ex-colleague because of Charlotte, his sister. Charlotte was completely different to Woody: she was unpredictable, impulsive, reckless and infuriating.

"You can do this," Angus muttered, and forced himself out of the car.

"All right mate!" Woody opened the front door with a wide smile. He was wearing bright-red shorts and a white T-shirt. "It's good to see you. Come through – you all right to sit in the garden?" He beckoned him in.

Angus wiped his feet thoroughly on the mat, a delaying tactic. "Yeah, sure." He followed Woody through to the garden, where there was a table and chairs with a parasol casting shade on half the patio area.

Woody waved at a chair, "Take a seat. I was just thinking about having a beer, you want one? I've got zero-alcohol ones, seeing as you're driving."

Angus sat in one of the shaded chairs. "That would be great. Thanks."

Woody went into the house, returned with two open bottles of beer and handed the non-alcoholic one to Angus. He sat in the chair next to Angus and took a swig. "So what can I do for you?"

Angus sipped his beer, musing that Woody never bothered with the niceties when they met up. No "How are you?" or "Nice weather we're having."

He decided to jump straight in. "I came to tell you about my latest client. It's Liam Beckett."

There was a moment of deathly silence as Woody processed the news. "Really?" He tilted his head slightly, then drank from his bottle.

"Yes. I wanted to tell you before I started the case. He wants me to prove he's innocent."

Woody's eyes narrowed a little. "Yeah, he was always banging on about his innocence." Woody upended his bottle again. "Not sure why you'd want to get involved with that lowlife. I take it Charlie's helping you?" Woody was the only one who called his sister Charlie, because he knew it annoyed her.

"She will be, yes. She said she would check that you didn't murder me when I told you."

Woody chuckled. "Don't worry, mate, I won't kill you.

Beckett's really clutching at straws, though. All the evidence points to his guilt – all of it. The CPS told me off the record that it was one of the clearest cases they'd had in a long time."

"And yet he wants to spend every penny he has paying for me to prove his innocence. He'd have fewer years on his sentence if he'd pleaded guilty."

Angus watched Woody's face. His relaxed face tightened, and he clenched his jaw. The warmth in his eyes vanished, replaced by an intense, laser-like focus. "That's true. Beckett thought the jury would side with him; it was close at one point, I'm told. I wasn't there when he gave evidence, and they took long enough to decide their verdict."

There was a long silence as Angus debated what to say next. "Do you think they made the right decision?"

Woody met his eyes. "From the evidence, yeah. I hope you're not implying there was other evidence I didn't investigate that would have proved his innocence."

"I worked with you long enough to know you'd never do that. But you must have had a idea of whether you thought he'd done it."

Woody blinked slowly, nodding approval of what Angus had asked. "He never broke. In the interviews, I mean. You know how it is? After a while their stories are inconsistent: they change and you know you can get them. His story never changed. But you noticed that already, didn't you?" Woody grimaced.

Angus wanted to ask why Woody hadn't explored that further. If he'd been in charge of the case, he'd have worked on that more. But then he remembered the pressure-cooker atmosphere of the police: cases piling up, lack of time, and reduced manpower to deal with it all. It was one of the many reasons why he'd left. "I did, and that's one of the main reasons why I'm taking the case."

"Well, despite that, we couldn't find anyone else with a reason to kill Brian. In the end, though, it was down to the CPS to prosecute, and the rest is history." Woody put his beer bottle on the table. "I won't be much help to you, though."

"Oh?"

"Not like that – I'm not angry. What I mean is that I can't remember much more than the basics. It's all in the reports and evidence, though: I'm a stickler for recording everything. Anyway, how did Charlotte react to me being on the case?"

The mention of Charlotte reminded Angus of her reaction the day before. "She's very anxious about what this case might do to your relationship."

That made Woody chuckle. "Nothing to do with her. It's between me and you."

There was a hint of roughness in Woody's voice, and Angus knew he was more annoyed than he was letting on. On the one hand, he wanted to get to the truth and hopefully prove Liam innocent. On the other, it would keep their friendship on an even keel if he didn't.

Angus examined the label on his beer bottle, pondering how to ask the other question that had been on his mind since he arrived. "Talking of Charlotte, what do you buy a multi-millionaire for her birthday? It's coming up soon and it's causing me a lot of worry."

"Changing the subject? Not very subtle, mate." Woody stared at him, a glint of amusement in his eye.

"What do you get her, though?"

Woody stretched his legs out and crossed them at the ankles. "You mean, what do you buy a woman who can buy herself anything she wants, has everything she already wants, and tells you she doesn't want anything for her birthday?" He gave a small chuckle and shook his head. "Welcome to my world. Yeah, I feel your pain. You have to get her something, don't you? Flowers, usually. She's a sucker for them. Since she's been loaded, it's been a bloody nightmare to get her anything. She always says she doesn't want anything but she always loved opening gifts."

Angus thought about the flowers her friend Ross had brought her when he'd visited not so long ago. Pink roses. If Ross had got her flowers, he'd have to do something better than that.

"I noticed she has jewellery from Tiffany." Angus had noticed a lot of it recently. Earrings, then a necklace and matching bracelet.

"Yeah, when she was a teenager she made me watch *Breakfast at Tiffany's* with her once. She was obsessed with it for a while, so it's no surprise that she's bought herself a load of Tiffany jewellery. Her watch is Cartier, you know? Well, when she's not wearing her smart watch."

Angus felt a lump in his throat. He did know. Charlotte literally did have everything she wanted. He took another swig of beer and wished it had some alcohol in it. This was going to be very tricky.

He saw Woody watching his reaction. "Try not to feel too bad," he said. "Charlie always says she doesn't want anything, but she likes even a small gift to open. You know that friend of hers, Ross?"

Angus inclined his head. "I met him not so long ago. He dropped in on her when I was staying there because of the World War Two bomb."

"He bought her a speedboat last birthday."

Angus nearly choked on his beer. Some of it landed on his shirt, and he brushed it away as he coughed.

"I know. She gets seasick, too." Woody laughed. "Not sure what Ross was thinking of, getting her that. Just shows, though. You can have a billion pounds and still get someone the wrong present."

Angus tried to suppress a feeling of foreboding. Maybe flowers would be best after all.

There was a long pause before Woody spoke again. "Look, as far as I'm concerned, that case is over. You know what it's like? We present the evidence, the CPS decide. If you want to look into it, you won't get any hassle from me. I haven't got time to go over old cases though."

"Thanks. I don't need your blessing to take the case, but I'm glad I have it."

Chapter Four

Angus drove home not long afterwards and had barely got through the front door when Charlotte called. Angus wondered whether she still had a tracking app on his phone.

"What did Mark say?" she demanded the moment he answered.

Angus walked into the kitchen. "Don't worry, he's fine with us taking the case. He thinks we're wasting our time, but you don't need to worry. He won't kill us or hinder us."

"Really? I thought he'd get the hump, or at least shout a bit."

"No, he took it well, but he said that he thinks on balance, Liam was guilty."

"Well, maybe he's right, maybe he's wrong. At least we can get going, then. Although shouldn't you tell Liam about me?"

Angus leaned against the kitchen counter. "I'll have to at some point, but for now I won't. You'll be impartial and look at the facts, just like me."

There was a long silence. "Of course I will. I think you

should tell him sooner rather than later, but you're the boss. Are you coming over?"

"Tomorrow. I'll get all the paperwork together and we can start then."

He ended the call, made a cup of tea, then took out his notebook and started to make a list of potential presents. *Flowers.* His pen hovered over the notepad. That was all he could think of. There must be something else.

After hearing about Charlotte's Tiffany and Cartier purchases, then the speedboat Ross had bought her, whatever he got would be embarrassing, pathetic, or both.

Maybe something to do with her philanthropic or charity work?

Donation to one of her causes or something similar, he wrote next.

Yes, maybe she'd like that. He'd heard about all sorts of charities where you could buy a goat or chickens for people in third-world countries in someone else's name.

He took out his phone and started to search, then stopped when he found an article warning that such gifts, although popular and well-meaning, could put strain on water supplies in some countries. Maybe there was something else...

The next morning, Angus sat in Charlotte's study. Charlotte sat poised at her desk, waiting for him to start the meeting. She looked fresh-faced and attentive. She was always so enthusiastic about a new case that it was endearing.

"I'm excited," she commented, watching Angus sort the current paperwork from the case. He'd brought over all the witness statements and the other evidence he'd received from the lawyers.

"If we're going to get to the truth," he said, "we need to make sure we're methodical. I've been thinking about this. If we're going to try and prove Liam innocent, we need to assume he is, even if everything points to him."

"All right." Charlotte gave a determined nod. "Where do we start?"

Angus tapped the papers. "Liam's lawyers have sent us their case notes, the court transcripts and anything else they think we should have. We need to read through it all and familiarise ourselves with it."

Charlotte leaned back in her chair. "What did his lawyers say to you?"

Angus shrugged. "Not much. They were a little surprised that Liam has hired us, but helpful. That is their job, though."

Charlotte pointed to the conspiracy board. "As you can see, I've put Liam and Brian's photos on the board. I'm not sure what else to put on, though. We don't have any other suspects."

"Not yet, but we will. We need to find evidence of anyone who might have a reason to want Brian dead. We must look into the victim's life thoroughly. The answer lies there, I'm sure of it."

"Shouldn't we look into why Liam wanted him dead first?"

Angus shook his head. "We're assuming he's innocent. It was a case of next-door neighbours with a longstanding dispute. Liam stated that their feud started four years before the murder."

"And?"

"And that was enough for them to fall out."

Charlotte screwed up her nose. "That's literally nothing."

"Neighbourly feuds usually start with not much at all. I dealt with my fair share of disputes when I was in uniform."

"What happened next?"

"The complaints escalated. Brian complained about noise from Liam's house. They argued about the front-garden boundary."

"Wait, what?"

Angus walked over to the table, riffled through the papers and pulled out a document with a plan of Liam and Brian's houses. "Their houses were semi-detached, on the site of a derelict farm. Their front gardens didn't have any fence defining the boundary, but the back gardens did."

"Were theirs the only houses there?"

Angus turned the plan around for Charlotte to see. "Yes. Just Liam and Brian's houses, which were old farm workers' cottages, two large barns, and the old farmhouse, which is a shell." He pointed to each of the buildings. The wider area showed nothing but fields. About half a mile away was a hamlet, more of a thoroughfare, and to the north of their houses a country estate and mansion.

Charlotte shook her head a little, making her blonde curls quiver. "Why was the farmhouse left like that, and the farm abandoned?"

"About twenty years before the tenant farmers had left. According to the landowner, Lord Farnley, the farm-house needed extensive work: so much so that he couldn't afford to renovate it. The land surrounding the farm was rented to sheep farmers and the farmhouse left uninhab-ited. But he must have found the money from somewhere because eventually he got planning permission for Liam and Brian's houses to be rebuilt as farm workers' houses a few years before. One was sold to Liam, the other rented to Brian."

Charlotte pointed to the mansion. "Is that Lord Farnley's house?"

"Yes. Sterling Hall."

"All that countryside around them, and they couldn't get past their hatred of the person next door. I have a good relationship with my neighbours here." Charlotte picked up a pen and tapped the end against her lips. "I mean, we rub along nicely. I don't see them much, though. One of them is in Australia half the year."

"All right for some," said Angus. "Anyway, it seems that living so close together with no one else around made them hate each other. Incident after incident was reported to the police. Both were as bad as each other."

"What sort of incidents?"

"I want to have a look at the houses. I'll go through the list when we get there."

"But what got Liam convicted? Surely they couldn't prove that he killed Brian from yet another argument between them that day?"

"The evidence that it was Liam was circumstantial to start with. Brian had gone to the pub after work: he was a gamekeeper for Lord Farnley. Witnesses in the pub said he left there at about 7pm. He went home. Then, at about 8pm, Liam knocked on his door and accused him of throwing dog poo into his garden, and they'd had a blazing row. Liam said Brian denied it, he punched him, then after a tussle, Liam went back in his house because of his nosebleed. Brian was murdered between 11pm and 1am. He was stabbed in his bed while he was sleeping."

Charlotte gasped. "That's horrible."

Angus put his hands in his pockets. "Yes."

"God, if I'd known that before I met Liam, I'm not sure I could have kept quiet."

"Remember, he says he's innocent. The evidence that secured his conviction was a fragment of his gardening over-alls, found in the incinerator in his back garden. Traces of Brian's blood were found on it. So there was both circumstantial and forensic evidence that he did it."

"Who murders someone, then burns the bloodstained clothes in their own back garden?" Charlotte grimaced. "I'd have taken them into the woods and burnt them there. It's too obvious."

"The evidence is damning," Angus acknowledged.

"And yet here we are taking on the case. Are you sure it's the right thing to do?"

Angus stared at the conspiracy board. "Yes."

Chapter Five

The drive from Charlotte's house in Topsham to the edge of Dartmoor, where Liam and Brian's houses were, took nearly an hour. They took Angus's black VW Golf and Charlotte navigated with the satnav on her phone. They bumped down a long farm lane to the buildings.

When Angus pulled up outside, Charlotte peered out of the window. "This is so bleak. The houses look as if they haven't been lived in for ages. I mean, look at those weeds in the front garden. It's practically a jungle."

Angus undid his seatbelt and followed her gaze. "They haven't been lived in for nearly a year, that's why. Brian is dead and Liam's in prison. Come on, let's walk around."

Outside, the sky was overcast and the light dull. Charlotte zipped up her jacket and was glad she'd worn extra-thick tights under her black and white striped skater dress.

They paused, taking in the atmosphere and gazing at the two brick semi-detached houses in front of them. "Which is Liam's?" Charlotte asked.

"The one on the left." Angus pointed. "He's had all his

belongings removed, and he intends to sell the house if he needs to, to cover our costs."

"Not much point going inside Liam's house, is there? But we should have a look inside Brian's, I suppose." Charlotte gave an involuntary shiver at the thought of viewing a murder scene. "Are we allowed to go in? There's no one living in the house, is there?"

Angus glanced at her. "Both houses are empty since the murder. Apparently no one wants to live in a house where there was murder, or next door to it. I haven't asked permission, but I do want to look inside Brian's house, or at least peep through the windows. He was murdered in the bedroom upstairs."

"Are you about to trespass?" Charlotte couldn't help smiling.

"It's only trespass if the landowner finds out. I'm sure Lord Farnley will be snug in his manor house."

"So Brian rented from Lord Farnley?"

"Yes and no. It was a grace-and-favour house from Lord Farnley, part of Brian's contract as a gamekeeper."

They walked to the front of Brian's house. A path went around the side, and Angus went to the front window and peered in. Charlotte followed. "There's no furniture."

"Brian's belongings were taken by his daughter."

They made their way round to the back garden. It was mainly lawn, but overgrown to knee height, with some species of grass stretching higher. Then they peered through the patio door.

"This is the living room," said Angus. "Whoever murdered him could have come through this door. There's no furniture in there, either." He tried to open the door, but it didn't budge. Then he looked inside again. "I've studied the murder scene photos, but I'd really like to see inside."

"Can you jimmy the door?"

"Probably, but I don't want to break the lock. And I'm not going to trespass. When we visit Lord Farnley, I'll ask if we can look inside."

Angus looked around the back garden, then examined the hedge between the two properties. A few minutes later he returned to Charlotte, who'd stayed by the house. "You were going to tell me about the list of complaints that Liam and Brian made during their feud," she commented.

Angus delved into his inside jacket pocket, took out a piece of paper and handed it to Charlotte. Charlotte read it out. "Liam: playing his music too loud, banging doors, parking too close to Brian's house, leaving his wheelie bin and recycling boxes outside in the street all the time. Brian: moving Liam's bins without permission, looking through Liam's windows when he wasn't in, setting his garden sprinkler so that it sprayed onto Liam's garden, burning leaves every Sunday... Oh God, it's annoying when people do that. Burning coal instead of smokeless fuel. That's annoying too, and illegal now." Charlotte shook her head. "Wow, they really had it in for one another."

Angus nodded. "But enough to kill? It's all very petty and stressful, but if Liam did kill Brian, what tipped him over the edge? There has to be a reason."

"Maybe he just flipped. Maybe he'd just had enough."

"That's possible, but in his statements, Liam said he was not under more stress over this situation than before."

Charlotte handed the paper back to Angus. "Did my brother find anything?"

"Nothing more. But Liam could be lying about the argument and its cause."

Charlotte sighed. "And Liam said he didn't notice anyone visiting Brian after the row."

"That's right. He said he went into his house and tried to calm down by playing loud music. Then he put the TV on and tried to stop thinking about the dispute. Come on, let's go home." They walked back to the car.

"What next, though?" asked Charlotte. "Starting a list of people who might have a reason to kill Brian?"

"Yes. I want to talk to his daughter first: she'll be able to help with that. She hasn't been answering my calls."

"She probably doesn't want to talk to someone who's trying to get her father's murderer off the hook." Charlotte said dryly.

Angus leaned against his car. "I get that. But it won't stop me trying to get as much information out of her as I can. She lives in Okehampton. It's only a short drive from here."

"Let's go."

Chapter Six

Angus and Charlotte knocked on Jessica Letterman's front door twenty minutes later but there was no answer. A local walking past told them that she worked as a teaching assistant at the local primary school, so they waited a short time, until the school day had ended and most of the children had left, before going to the school's reception and asking to speak to her.

The large, middle-aged woman behind the window told them to wait where they were. She raised her eyebrows when Angus said their visit was personal and not to do with the school.

"What is it about the smell of school?" Charlotte said, as they waited. "I went to school in Hertfordshire and my boys did too, and the smell here is exactly the same. It brings back lots of horrible memories of being bullied by Phillip Davies. He was a little shit of a boy."

Angus glanced at her. "I take it you found him on the internet?"

"You know me too well," Charlotte gave him a mischievous smile. "And no, I didn't hack him or do anything to

29

hurt him. It's all water under the bridge. The things we do as children shouldn't define us as adults. He works as a plumber and he's married with two girls. He's also big and bulky, and looks older than mid-forties."

Angus chuckled. "Remind me never to get on your wrong side."

"You've said that before."

"I know, but I need constant reminders."

A door at the side of the office opened and a woman appeared. She was about thirty, dressed in black leggings and an oversized blue and silver checked shirt, with long brown hair in a ponytail. She was slim, with an energetic demeanour. Angus, who was standing, stepped towards her. "Jessica Letterman? I'm Angus Darrow and this is my colleague, Charlotte."

Charlotte smiled, but noted that Angus had again used just her first name.

"Yes, how can I help?" said Jessica.

Angus glanced at the receptionist, who was shuffling papers but not doing anything with them. "Is there somewhere we can talk privately? This is a personal matter."

Jessica looked puzzled but nodded. "Sure, we can go to the staff room. But you'll have to sign in first." She pointed to the visitors' book on the counter. Angus and Charlotte signed in and followed her through a door into the staff room. It was a small room with two worn old sofas and a coffee table in the middle. At the side was a bench cluttered with mugs, a kettle, and canisters holding tea and coffee. There was also a sink and cupboards.

"Take a seat." Angus and Charlotte sat on one sofa, with Jessica opposite. "What's this about?"

Angus cleared his throat. "We're private investigators looking into your father's murder."

Jessica frowned. "Why? They found his killer – it was that bastard Liam Beckett. I hope he's rotting in prison." The frown deepened. "Wait a minute, are you TikTok detectives or something? I've heard about them. Real-life snoopers who think they can solve murders."

Angus shifted in his seat, making the sofa's old springs move Charlotte as well as himself. "We've been hired to look into whether he was actually guilty."

"Who by? Anyway, he *was* guilty. I was in court every day during his trial. He might have denied it, but everything pointed to him."

"We've been hired by Liam Beckett himself."

"What?" Jessica scowled and leaned forward. "You're joking, right? You've seriously come here to talk to me about this?"

Charlotte spoke in a soft tone. "Liam has always maintained he's innocent. We just want to get to the truth."

"The truth? The truth is that that bastard killed my Dad. My only parent, and you want me to help you get him off the hook? You've got some barefaced cheek, coming here and expecting me to help you!" Jessica's face started to flush.

Charlotte met Jessica's eyes. "It is unusual, I know, but just for a minute, please think about whether Liam might actually be innocent. Would you want him sitting in prison when he's done nothing wrong, and all the time the real killer is out there?"

"He's sitting in prison because he killed Dad! A court convicted him. He took Dad from me." Jessica covered her face with her hands and started to cry, her whole body shaking.

Charlotte glanced at Angus, who nodded, and she moved to sit next to Jessica. "Look, I know we're probably the last people you want to see, but we're just trying to find out if there was anyone else who might have wanted him dead."

Jessica slowly took her hands from her face. Her eyes were red from crying.

Angus went over to the kitchen bench, picked up a roll of kitchen towel and handed Jessica a piece. She wiped her eyes, then blew her nose. "I can't help. He had lots of mates down the pub, but that's all. There was no one else who wanted to kill him."

"Are you sure about that?" Angus sat on the sofa facing her.

"I'm sure. Can you go now, please. I've been trying to heal after what happened, and this isn't helping."

Angus glanced at Charlotte; his expression showed that he wasn't finished. "When was the last time you saw your dad before he was killed?"

"It was about a week before. He came over for Sunday lunch."

"Did he visit every week?"

"No. Once a month, maybe. Most times we'd go to a pub, but that time he came to me. He probably wanted to get away from Liam Beckett and all the terrible things he did." Her voice was bitter. "Please, go now. I'm not answering any more questions."

The staff-room door opened and the receptionist came in. "Everything all right, Jess?"

"No. These two are working for that bastard Liam. They're trying to get him off the hook."

The receptionist turned to them, Eyes blazing, her face transformed into a grimace of fury. "You two need to sling your hook. Talk about rubbing salt in the wound. After all she's been through, now this."

Angus and Charlotte stood up. "Thank you for your time," Angus said. "I'm sorry to have distressed you, but we're only on the side of truth." He took a business card from his pocket and handed it to her. "If you change your mind about talking, give me a call."

Outside, it was quiet. All the children and parents had left.

"She didn't react as badly as I thought she would," Angus said, as they walked to the car.

"Really? What exactly were you trying to get from her?"

"Just some information about Brian. You know, an idea about him as a person, apart from what we have in all the reports. It could have saved us some time, but at least we tried."

"What do we do now?"

"We go home and start again tomorrow. We'll have to see if we can find anyone else who knew him. I want to talk to his friends in the pub, at the very least."

They got into the car and put on their seatbelts. Angus looked at his watch. "I should be back in time for the running club 10K."

"You've joined a running club?"

"I have." He started the engine and the radio came on in the background with an over played pop song. "Exe Runners. I decided I needed to try and get out a bit more. Mix with people. You know?"

"Made many friends?" Charlotte tried to keep the jealousy out of her voice.

"A few. It's a big club. They have runs every night of the week, and at the weekend."

"You don't run every night, though?"

"No, just once a week so far."

"I have plans too tonight," Charlotte said quickly. "I'm starting a new hobby."

"Really? What is it?"

"Promise not to laugh?"

Angus nodded.

"Helena suggested I try something with my hands, and seeing as one of my favourite TV programs is *Pottery Throw Down*..."

"You're trying pottery?"

"I am."

"I haven't done that since school," Angus said. "I was terrible."

"Same here, but I'm giving it a go."

"Is Helena going too?"

"No. Just me."

Angus glanced at her. "Let me know how it goes."

"Don't worry." She grinned. "I won't be making dodgy pots and giving them to you as presents."

Chapter Seven

That evening, Charlotte stepped into the pottery workshop on Gandy Street in the centre of Exeter. It was a cafe and workshop during the day, where you could have coffee and cake while glazing a piece of pottery to be fired and collected later. They ran pottery classes too, and Charlotte had opted for the evening class rather than give up her time with Angus during the day.

She'd seen an advert for the classes in a Facebook group and her interest had been piqued when it mentioned using a pottery wheel. She'd always wanted to try one, and as she had mentioned to Angus earlier, she watched *Pottery Throw Down* religiously. The show, where ordinary people made all sorts of different pieces to compete for the top prize, was something Charlotte watched as a distraction once a week.

The cafe was deserted, but as soon as the old-fashioned bell above the door rang, a man's face appeared from behind a door at the back. "Hello!" he said. "Here for the class?"

Charlotte closed the door behind her and walked forward. "Yes. I'm Charlotte Lockwood."

The man was about fifty and despite having more grey hair than brown, he was tall and slim with an angular, handsome face. "Come through, come through." He beckoned her enthusiastically, a bright smile on his face. Charlotte couldn't help but do as he asked.

In the back of the cafe were two other students. One was a large grey-haired woman of about sixty, dressed in a frumpy brown skirt, a white T-shirt and a bobbly cream cardigan. She held a mug of tea in one hand. Next to her was a man of at least seventy, bespectacled and grey haired, in brown cord trousers and a black T-shirt.

"I'm David," said the man who'd greeted her. He indicated the vacant chair and Charlotte sat down. "Can I offer you a coffee, or would you prefer tea?"

Charlotte hesitated. She still wasn't sure about accepting drinks from strangers after what had happened in a previous case, but David seemed naturally open and friendly. "Tea would be lovely. Milk, no sugar."

"Great." David clapped his hands together. "You all introduce yourselves and get to know each other. I'll be back in a jiffy."

David disappeared through a side door and Charlotte turned to the others. "I'm Charlotte."

"Maggie," said the woman, then took a sip of her drink.

"Dennis." The man nodded to her. Silence fell.

"Nice weather lately." Maggie pulled her cardigan around her middle. It didn't quite reach.

"Yes!" Charlotte said, out of desperation. "Although it is June, usually the hottest month of the year, so it's not altogether surprising." She hated small talk about the weather. It was always such an obvious subject to talk about when you had nothing else to say. Dennis stared at the opposite wall, seemingly ignoring them both.

There was another awkward silence before Charlotte realised it was her turn to start the conversation. "Have you been to a class here before, Maggie?" she asked.

Maggie's expression lit up. "Oh yes, plenty of times. I love it. Can't stay away." She laughed. "I'm terrible, though. That's why I'm back. Poor David, he's lovely about it, but he must despair of my terrible work."

Charlotte glanced at Dennis, who was still staring at nothing. "I'm sure he doesn't mind an enthusiastic student. What about you, Dennis?"

Dennis turned his head like a crane and looked at her through his steel-framed glasses. "I used to work in a pottery factory when I was a teenager and I thought I'd try it again."

Charlotte nodded. "Where was that?"

"Stoke-on-Trent." Dennis turned away and stared into the distance again. Charlotte wondered whether going for a run with Angus would have been a better option.

"Here we are!" David came back in carrying a mug of tea and handed it to Charlotte. He sat down in the only spare chair, so that they were in a sort of circle. "Right." He put his hands on his knees and grinned. "I'm really excited to get you all pottering!" He laughed. "Maggie, you know what we'll be doing. Dennis and Charlotte, I'll guide you through everything you need to know."

Two hours later, Charlotte stood at the sink, washing the clay from her hands. David had been an attentive and enthusiastic teacher, and she'd tried the pottery wheel. It had been a disaster to start with, but with David's enthusiasm she could see why Maggie kept coming back for more. The pottery she had produced was completely awful, but she'd had fun – and best of all, it had been without using a computer or screen. She could see why Helena had suggested something offline.

"Bye, Dennis," David said in the cafe area, then came back through. "It takes a while to get the clay off, but it's worth the hassle when you create something you're proud of."

Charlotte continued scrubbing under her nails. "It'll be a while before that happens," she said drily.

He smiled. "As long as you had fun."

"I did," she conceded, although she didn't like being bad at anything except cooking. But she hated that so it was different.

Maggie, standing at the other sink, turned off the tap, dried her hands, then picked up a board with some kind of demented-looking clay animal on it and took it to David. "What do you think? Am I getting even a tiny bit better?"

He inspected it. "It's much better, Maggie. We'll get you on *Throw Down* soon enough."

Maggie grinned, and Charlotte thought she blushed a little.

David pointed to the other side of the room. "Put it over there, and I'll fire it as soon as it's dry."

Maggie did what she was told and Charlotte dried her hands. "What are we going to do next week?" she asked.

David raised his eyebrows and grinned, "We'll try making our first proper plant pot. You'll get to glaze it the week after that."

"Sounds great."

Chapter Eight

The next morning, it was back to business. Angus and Charlotte were in her study, coffees in hand, studying the conspiracy board.

In the middle was a photo of Brian, the victim. To the left was a photo of Liam with 'convicted neighbour' underneath.

Charlotte walked towards the board with a printed photo of Brian's daughter, from what Angus thought was one of her social media accounts. "How was the run last night?" she asked, pinning the photo of Jessica near Brian.

Angus watched her over his mug. "Good. Perfect weather for it, and there were at least thirty people. Some of us went to the pub afterwards; they're a good bunch. How was pottery?"

Charlotte returned to her chair. "It was good. I was terrible at it – using a wheel is much harder than it looks – but I enjoyed it. The tutor was very patient with me." There was a long pause before Charlotte indicated the conspiracy board. "What's next with the case?"

"We still need to concentrate on looking into Brian's life

and finding someone who might have a reason to want him dead."

"So we need to look into his life before he was murdered...Could Liam help with that?"

"I've requested a phone call with him at the prison but it will take a few days. I doubt he knew much about his private life though. In the meantime, we need to go over the police reports and the witness statements."

"Couldn't we just ask my brother?"

Angus shook his head. "I don't want to bother Woody unless there's no other option. He's been very good about us taking on this case, and he said he doesn't remember much anyway. He'd also tell us he's looked into everything already and check his notes and reports. He's excellent at his job."

"But we need to leave no stone unturned." She sighed. "All right, give me some of the reports and I'll start reading."

Angus went over to the piles of paper, picked out the relevant reports and gave half to Charlotte.

A few hours later, they'd built up a profile of Brian and his life. Charlotte had created a display on the study wall with information about him as they found it.

They reviewed everything. Angus went over the list they'd collated. "Brian worked for Lord Farnley as a game-keeper. Lord Farnley was also his landlord, and Brian had been there five years. He sometimes went to the pub half a mile away, walking there after work, and most often ordering a meal. He usually sat on his own at the bar but knew a few of the regulars. He didn't have any hobbies, except for winding up Liam, his next-door neighbour." He huffed out a breath. "His daughter was right: he didn't have much of a social life at all outside the pub."

"We definitely need to speak to Lord Farnley and the pub landlord too, don't you think? If we don't get any info from them, and hopefully they can point us to his pub friends. What then?"

"We'll cross that bridge when we come to it. I'll get in touch with Lord Farnley to see when we can meet him and in the meantime, we can drop into the pub."

Charlotte looked at her watch. "How about now?"

"All right, we can have lunch there. If we're paying customers, the landlord might be more willing to talk."

Chapter Nine

When they arrived at the Hare and Hounds pub they stood outside for a moment, admiring the picture-postcard building with its thatched roof, whitewashed walls and blooming hanging baskets. It was quintessentially English and Angus guessed it was at least a few hundred years old, if not older.

Inside it was quiet, with just one table occupied. They chose a table by one of the windows.

"What are you going to have?" Charlotte's eyes darted over the menu, then she passed it to Angus. It had typical pub food: burgers, cottage pie, ham, egg and chips, sausages and mash, ploughman's lunch and chicken tikka masala.

He read the menu. "Steak and ale pie."

"I'm going to go for the fish and chips."

"That sounds tempting, but I had that last night at the pub with the running club."

Charlotte had been looking at the bar, and turned quickly towards him. Her eyes were slightly narrowed. Why was that? Annoyance? The bright sunshine outside? He couldn't be sure.

She stood up. "I'll order at the bar. What drink?"

He motioned to her to sit back down. "I'll go. I want to sound out the landlord, to see if he'll be open to answering questions about Liam and Brian."

Charlotte sat down. "Fine, you're the lead investigator. I'll have a lime and soda water."

Angus went to the bar. The barman was filling one of the bar fridges with bottles of J2O and turned around when he spotted him. "What can I get you?" Angus guessed the man was in his early sixties. He was at least six foot two.

Angus ordered and paid for the drink and meals, then decided to open the conversation. "Are you the landlord?" he asked.

"Yeah, that's me. William."

"How long have you been here?"

"Coming up to eight years now. I like it here. There's a good community spirit."

"That's quite some time. I bet you've seen a few dramas. Is it true this is the pub Brian Letterman came to before he was murdered?"

The man paused for a moment, his eyebrows raised as he processed what Angus had just said. "Yeah, that's right. He used to come here several times a week. He was well liked."

"Did he have many friends?"

William put both his hands on the bar. "A few. Generally blokes who live nearby and come in most nights for a pint or two, to get out of the house. You know how it is. Although Brian was single, he'd come here for food. Couldn't be bothered to cook for one."

Angus nodded. "Terrible what happened to him. Did he have much of a social life, besides coming here?"

William shook his head. "Nah. He was the sort of bloke

who liked his own company, you know? Worked hard, went home or came here, back at work the next day. He liked football, though. He was a Plymouth Argyle supporter, which got him a lot of grief – most of us are loyal to Exeter City. There was a bit of banter, but nothing else."

"Did he go to matches?"

"Nah. He either watched here or at home. Paid the extortionate fee for the sports channels on satellite TV." The landlord shook his head. "I pay it too, but it's for the punters."

"What about Liam Beckett? Did he come in here too?"

The landlord's face darkened. "Sometimes. Not usually when Brian was here, because they hated each other."

"It was a shock, what happened."

"Yeah, terrible. Poor Brian. He didn't deserve that."

Angus decided he couldn't really ask any more without arousing the landlord's suspicions. "Thanks for these." Angus picked up their drinks and went back to Charlotte, who was looking at her mobile phone. When he sat down, she put it away. "You know, we've been investigating for three days and I haven't hacked anyone's Wi-Fi!" Charlotte picked up her glass and took a sip.

Angus shifted in his seat. "Who would you have hacked by now?"

"Jessica's home, this pub, Brian's employer."

Angus chuckled. "Just a few, then. How are you coping with it? Or rather, without it?"

Charlotte sat back in her seat. "Fine for now, but you know that at some point it'll come in very handy, and then you'll regret banning me. What did the barman say when you questioned him? Is he the landlord?"

Angus updated her. "He had a few friends here, liked

football, just an ordinary bloke really." The door opened and Angus watched a couple in their sixties go to the bar.

Their meal arrived fifteen minutes later. Charlotte's fish and chips filled the plate, and the crispy batter surrounding the fish was fluffy and light. Angus's steak and ale pie sat on a pile of mashed potato and gravy. They ate in companionable silence for a while.

"Do you think we should find out who Brian's friends were?" said Charlotte, between mouthfuls. "I know they weren't close, but they might know something."

Angus had just put a forkful of pie and mash in his mouth, and it was a few seconds before he could speak. "Don't worry. Before we leave, I'll ask him that very question. I wasn't going to leave without finding out."

"Good."

When they'd finished eating, Angus went back to the bar. "Another drink?" asked the landlord.

Angus shook his head. "Thanks for the food, it was great. I was wondering who Brian's friends in the pub were."

William's eyes narrowed. "You're asking a lot of questions about Brian, you are. He needs to rest in peace, while that bastard who kills him rots in prison. Are you a journalist or something?"

"No, I'm just interested in finding out more about Brian."

"I haven't got anything else to say about him."

Charlotte came up to stand beside Angus, sighed, then took out her purse and extracted a small pile of notes.

Angus stared at her, wide-eyed.

Charlotte held up the notes. "Would this help to persuade you otherwise?"

William stared at the money. "Add a bit more and it will."

Charlotte added a few more twenty-pound notes to the pile and put it on the bar. "The names of his friends here..."

He picked up the money and began counting it. "Ben Morgan, he lives on West Street. Gary Reid, he's a farmer over the way."

"Is that all?"

He nodded. "Yeah. Pretty much. He didn't mix with anyone he worked with. He didn't like his boss Lord Farnley. Said he was a pain in the backside and never pleased with anything he did."

Charlotte pulled out Angus's notepad from his jacket pocket, opened it at an empty page, reached back into his pocket for a pen, then wrote the details in his pad. "Thank you. You've been very helpful and the food was lovely."

The landlord put the money into his jeans pocket. "Cheers. If you have time, I'd appreciate a good review on TripAdvisor."

Charlotte nodded, then took Angus's arm and led him to the exit.

Chapter Ten

Outside, she handed Angus his notepad and pen. "That was fruitful. And delicious. It's been ages since I've had fish and chips that good."

Angus stuffed his pad and pen into his pocket. "What was that?"

"What?"

"Bribes!"

Charlotte rolled her eyes. "You told me not to hack; you didn't ban me from bribing people. And he wasn't going to talk without an incentive. Everyone has their price, and he was cheap." There was a note of disgust in her voice. "Anyway Angus, stop being so controlling. I'm not hacking, and even the police use bribes to get information."

"From criminals, not the general public!" Angus could feel his face flushing with anger.

Charlotte walked towards the car, then turned. "Either way, we got the info. Let's try and speak to them."

Angus stood still, debating whether or not to continue the argument or relent. He shook his head, and started to walk to the car, speechless.

Charlotte sat in the passenger seat searching the internet for Ben and Gary. It didn't take her long to find them.

"Turn left out of the pub car park and Ben's house is about a quarter of a mile on the left." She didn't look up.

Angus started the car and obeyed, still seething with anger at her presumptuousness.

Ben's house was in a cul-de-sac off the main road. The modern houses looked as though they'd been built a few years ago with the aim of getting maximum capacity from the space allowed.

Angus parked in one of the visitor spaces. Ben's house was in the middle of a terrace of five. Angus knocked on the front door.

It was answered quickly. "Ben Morgan?" Angus asked.

"Yeah." Ben wore a dark-blue knitted jumper and light-blue jeans. He was a large man, his beer belly confirming that he spent time in the pub down the road.

"I'm Angus Darrow and this is my colleague, Charlotte. We're looking into the death of Brian Letterman. May we come in?"

Ben looked from Angus to Charlotte. "Brian? They found his killer, though."

"Could we come in and I'll explain."

Ben hesitated, then opened the door wider. "Er, OK."

Inside, the house was small. The kitchen was to the right and there was a single room downstairs: living and dining room combined. A three-seater sofa and matching armchair faced the TV and a fold-down table for two was pushed against the wall.

Ben indicated that they sit down. Angus went to the sofa and Charlotte sat next to him, while Ben took the chair. "Why are you looking into Brian's death, then?"

Angus took out his notebook. "We're private detectives, hired by Liam Beckett to look into who killed Brian."

"What?" Ben frowned and narrowed his eyes. "I know Liam said he was innocent, but he was found guilty."

Angus looked Ben in the eye. "He still maintains that he's innocent. Despite the conviction, we're exploring all avenues to find the truth – whatever it may be."

Ben shrugged. "If he wants to waste his money, that's his problem. You won't find anything the police didn't."

Angus gave Charlotte a sidelong glance at Ben's mention of the police. "I'd like to ask you some questions about Brian, if that's OK?"

"All right." Ben sat back in his chair and put his hands on the arms.

"You were a friend of Brian's?"

"Not a close one. We drank together at the pub a couple of times a week but it was all very casual. We didn't meet up outside that. We just chatted because we happened to be at the pub at the same time."

"So you didn't socialise together at all outside the pub?"

Ben shook his head.

"Not even once?"

"Nah. Brian was a bit of a hermit when he wasn't at the pub."

"What sort of things did Brian talk about in the pub?"

"You know, the usual. Football, the weather. Sometimes his work, but not often."

"Was he seeing anyone?"

"Don't think so. He never mentioned a bird."

Charlotte cleared her throat and turned away. Angus knew she was trying to hide her feelings about Ben's use of the term 'bird'.

"Was he gay?" she asked.

Ben turned to her. "Nah, he was straight. He'd ogle women when they walked in the pub. Couldn't help himself."

Angus took out his notebook. "How long had you been pub friends?"

Ben gazed into the distance, thinking. "About three years, I reckon. Not long after I moved into this house."

"Was Brian involved in any social activities, in the pub or anywhere else?"

Ben pursed his lips. "He came to the pub quiz now and then – he was good at answering the sports questions, and the wildlife ones too. He was a bit of a nature fan and ecowarrier in his own way. But outside, not a thing. If he did do anything, he never said. I still can't believe Liam Beckett's insisting he's innocent. I read the reports of the trial, and all the evidence pointed to him."

Angus shifted in his seat. "Did you know Liam before all this happened?"

Ben sighed. "No. I saw him about, that's all. He came into the pub occasionally, but I never spoke to him. I knew about his rift with Brian and the grief he gave him, so I didn't talk to him. Brian would tell us about it if we asked, but he said he came to the pub to get away from it all."

"What sort of things did Brian tell you?" Charlotte asked. "We've seen the police reports, but there must have been things that happened and didn't get reported."

"Oh yeah, there was loads. They both reported each other to the police, who came round plenty of times. It was Liam playing loud music that got to Brian the most. It was always in the early hours of the morning, when Brian was fast asleep. Liam would play heavy metal for about an hour. If Brian went round to complain, Liam never answered the door because he couldn't hear him."

"Anything else?"

"There was so much that I can't even remember it all."

They sat in silence for a moment, then Ben continued. "A couple of times, Brian said Liam would shine a bright light into his windows. Then when he looked out, he'd switch it off. He also said that twice he'd had a flat tyre when he got to work, and he'd found a nail in the tyre."

Angus glanced at Charlotte as he wrote. "I hadn't heard of those, and I had an extensive list already."

Ben tilted his head to the side. "The weird thing was that a few weeks before Liam murdered Brian, they'd reached a sort of truce. They agreed to stop doing anything that annoyed the other. It was tentative to start with, but I could tell Brian was happy. It was as though a weight had been lifted from him. Then, after a couple of days, Liam started it up again. He threw dog waste into Brian's garden, and he poisoned the plants in his front garden with weedkiller. I mean, why couldn't he just let it be, you know?" Ben shook his head, then glared at them. "So the fact you're helping Liam, well, that tells me a lot about you two. Liam was a complete arsehole who was hell-bent on making Brian's life a misery. So much so that eventually he murdered him. And here *you* are helping him."

Angus took a deep breath and pushed his glasses up his nose. He understood why Ben felt that way. If he was in his position, he'd probably feel the same. "We want justice for Brian, whatever form that takes."

"But he was found guilty!" Ben cried. "I just don't understand why you would want to help Liam Beckett."

Charlotte leaned forward. "Look, Ben, just for a moment imagine that Liam is innocent and he's stuck in prison for a crime he didn't commit."

Ben stared at Charlotte. "But all the evidence was there."

"How well did Brian and Gary get on?" Angus asked, to change the subject.

Ben moved his gaze from Charlotte to Angus. "All right. They didn't argue. None of us did. Not with Brian."

"Was there anyone else in your pub social group?"

"Not really. Mary and Edward would occasionally chat, and sometimes Jim who runs the monthly folk club, but that was it. Brian didn't go to the folk club because Liam went sometimes."

"He didn't go to any other special events at the club?"

"No. Just the quizzes, like I said."

Angus closed his notepad and put it in his pocket, then stood up. Charlotte followed his lead. "Ben, thanks for talking to us. We appreciate it."

"All right," muttered Ben, and saw them out.

As soon as they were in the car, Charlotte vented her anger. "What a tosser he was, using the word 'bird'. It's so derogatory, and totally 1970s."

"That was polite, Charlotte. Some of the names men use for women between themselves are far worse."

Charlotte shook her head. "You'd never use that term and I'll bet you don't use the others, either. If other men were more like you, the world would be a much better place."

Angus smiled. "Thank you for the compliment."

Charlotte blushed. "He seemed pretty annoyed that we were working for Liam."

"He was nicer than I expected. Bringing up something like this is bound to cause friction. We have to focus on trying to find the truth."

"Should we find Gary next, seeing as we're over here?"

The evening was starting to draw in, but there was still an hour or so of daylight left.

Angus nodded. "Put his address in the sat nav and we'll go straight there."

Chapter Eleven

Gary's farm was more of a smallholding. The long drive that led to the house had numerous potholes, so Angus drove carefully, avoiding as many as he could. His VW Golf was built for well-kept roads in towns and cities.

"A 4x4 would be the best vehicle for this place," Charlotte commented.

"I'll consider one when I'm looking to replace this." Angus turned the steering wheel left, narrowly avoiding another pothole.

Gary's house was at the end of the drive, next to an old barn. The barn's corrugated-steel roof had several gaping holes and was held up by rusty steel poles. Half the barn was taken up by straw bales, the other half by scrap metal, tarpaulins, and farm machinery that looked as if it had been made decades ago.

As they pulled up next to a beaten up Ford estate, the front door opened and a man came out. He was wearing a green waxed jacket, jeans and black wellington boots.

"Gary?" Charlotte speculated.

"We'll see..." Angus stopped the car engine and got out. Charlotte followed.

"Gary Reid?" Angus asked as the man approached. He was in his mid-fifties, with a black beard and greying hair.

"Yeah. Are you the private detectives who just left Ben?"

Angus lifted his chin. Clearly, Ben had phoned Gary to fill him in. "Yes, can we talk?"

Gary put his hands in his pockets and widened his stance, his legs now slightly apart. "I haven't got anything to say to scumbags like you. Beckett shouldn't be allowed to get himself off the hook. The stupid bastard ought to rot in jail. Shame they got rid of the death penalty. I'd vote to bring it back for bastards like him."

Angus stood his ground and spoke in his calmest voice. "I understand you're upset, Gary, but we just want to ask you a couple of questions."

"Like what?" Gary narrowed his eyes.

"We're trying to find out more about Brian, and particularly his life leading up to the murder. What did he talk about when you met in the pub?

Gary scowled at him. "You're trying to catch me out, you are. So you can accuse me of killing him."

Angus shook his head. "That's not true. We're just trying to find out as much as possible about Brian."

Gary folded his arms. "It was just bloke chat." He shook his head, then glared at Angus. "Oh no, you won't get anything out of me. You can go back to Liam and tell him from me that he can go to hell. Now clear off!" He shouted the last part.

Angus turned to Charlotte. "Let's go."

They got into the car. Angus turned round and headed back down the lane. He could see Gary watching them. It seemed to take twice as long to get to the main road as it had to come down the drive.

They didn't speak for some time. Angus had automatically headed for Topsham to drop Charlotte off. It wasn't until they'd reached the A30 to Exeter that Angus spoke. "We'll need to go over the reports to see if Gary gave a statement."

"You think he's hiding something?"

"No. But if he won't talk to us, we'll have to find out about his relationship to Brian another way."

"I can't remember seeing his name in any of the reports."

"Me neither. But it's worth checking again."

When Angus pulled onto Charlotte's drive he kept the engine running. "Not coming in?" Charlotte asked.

"I'd better get back: I've an early start. Which reminds me, I won't be able to come over tomorrow. I've got to do some DIY at the flats, and a few other things."

"Sounds mysterious."

"It's not. Boring, everyday adult stuff, nothing to get excited about. We'll continue with the case the day after. Haven't you got a spa to go to?"

Charlotte grinned. "I always have a spa to go to."

"There you go."

"OK, see you the day after tomorrow. Thanks for lunch, by the way." She got out of the car and Angus drove off.

Chapter Twelve

The next day, Charlotte got up late. With Angus not due to arrive, she sat in bed considering whether to go to a spa and if so, which. In the end, she decided to treat herself to a bit of retail therapy and Grigore drove her into Exeter.

After browsing in a few shops she ended up in a second-hand bookshop at the bottom of Fore Street. She'd always preferred the wider choice in the secondhand bookshops, even since making her millions.

The bookshop was housed in a large old building tucked out of the way of most shoppers. The musty smell of the books hit her as soon as she entered, then it mixed with coffee and she spotted a small cafe area at the back. She made her way to the fiction section first, browsed the titles and chose a few. Then she wandered through to the non-fiction section and turned a corner to see David, the pottery tutor, holding a large map.

Charlotte approached him. "Hello!"

"Oh, hello. Fancy seeing you here." He smiled as he

tried to fold the map into its original form, but it didn't seem to want to cooperate.

"Here, let me help." Charlotte put her books down on a shelf. "I think it has to be folded here..." She folded it down and it concertinaed into place.

"Thanks." David grinned at her. "I thought I was going to have to buy it, just because I felt guilty about not getting it folded properly."

Charlotte laughed. "That would have been annoying."

David was wearing a dark-brown checked shirt and smart dark-blue jeans. He had a few days' worth of dark stubble, which gave him more of a casual look than when he'd taught her pottery.

Charlotte picked up her books from the shelf. "I'm just browsing. I can rarely leave a bookshop without buying at least one or two books."

"Murder-mystery fan, I see," David commented. "I know what you mean. I can't help buying books either. I've got the biggest 'to read' pile ever, and it's always growing."

"Me too."

Charlotte looked at the map he was holding and read out the title. "*Historical map of Hertfordshire.*"

"Yes. I grew up there and I've been looking at the 1921 census. I'm searching for where my grandparents lived. There's an online map, of course, but I prefer a paper one."

"Whereabouts in Hertfordshire? I grew up there too."

"Hemel Hempstead."

Charlotte smiled. "Really? I lived in Grovehill, the dodgy part!" She laughed, hoping he wouldn't think too badly of her.

"I was just up the road in Bennetts End."

"I know it well. What a coincidence! Which school did you go to? I went to Foxhills."

"So did I! Mind you, you look a fair bit younger than me, so I doubt we were there at the same time."

"I left in 1994."

"Well, I left in 1988, so we wouldn't have been there at the same time."

"Was Mr McGregor teaching when you were there?" Charlotte asked.

David took a deep, exaggerated breath. "Oh yes. He was scary, wasn't he? I used to dread history lessons."

"Me too." There was a long pause, and Charlotte heard the clink of cups in the back of the shop. "Would you like to grab a coffee? I was just about to get a bite to eat."

David smiled. "I'd love that."

They headed to the cafe area, grabbed a table, then ordered food and drinks.

"So what did you do when you left Foxhills?" Charlotte asked, stirring a spoonful of sugar into her coffee.

David leaned back in his chair. "Oh well, there's a story. I got a job in the City with one of the top banks. Stayed there for fifteen years." He paused. "I got married, but my wife died a couple of years later. I looked after her during her illness and it made me re-evaluate everything, you know?" He turned the saucer with his hand, looking down at it thoughtfully.

"Is that how you got into pottery?"

David looked up. "Not at first. I moved to Devon for six months to get away from all the memories, and it grew on me. Fifteen years later, I'm still here."

Charlotte chuckled. "Yes, Devon has that effect, doesn't it?"

"How did you end up down here, Charlotte?"

Charlotte sipped her coffee as she considered how much to tell David. "I used to work in London too, in computing. I moved down here when I got divorced. My brother lives in Exeter and I wanted to be near him and his wife."

"Computing, eh? Is that what you do now?"

"Yes." She pondered what else to say, and decided to tell a vague version of the truth. "I work for a local businessman as his assistant. He's a bit of a technophobe, so I help him with all his computer issues."

She looked David over. He was attractive, and he had a sort of vulnerability about him. His smile and his warmth were endearing. She glanced at his ring finger: no ring. That didn't mean he was completely single, but a part of her was hoping he was.

She took another sip of her coffee and her mind slipped away to Angus and the hopelessness of their situation. He just didn't seem interested in her, not in that way.

As they ate their sandwiches and drank coffee, they chatted about Hertfordshire, their schooldays, and how their lives had changed in Devon until David looked at his watch. "Can you believe we've been here a whole hour? I should go. I've got a lesson with Maggie soon."

"Maggie from the same lesson as me? She seems to like pottery a lot."

David chuckled, "Almost as much as me, which is a *lot*."

"Are you working tonight?" Charlotte found herself asking.

"Er, no. I'm not. I have no plans." He looked at her, a half-smile on his face.

"Would you like to have dinner? I've been meaning to try the Italian restaurant, the one near John Lewis. I hate eating alone."

There was a five-second pause which felt like five hours before David answered "I'd love that."

Chapter Thirteen

The next day, Angus arrived at 9.30am on the dot, and for the first time since the previous night, Charlotte had the tiniest of regrets that it was David, not Angus, that she'd shared a night of passion with. Angus looked particularly fetching in his suit today, and all her feelings for him which she kept in check came flooding back.

"Did you get everything done that you needed to yesterday?" she asked once they were in her study, coffees in hand.

Angus smiled. "No, but that's OK. I'll just have to do the same next week. What did you get up to yesterday? Anything exciting?"

Charlotte had just taken a sip of coffee and tried not to choke on it. "Er, I went into Exeter and did a bit of shopping. I went to that secondhand bookshop at the bottom of Fore Street for a browse."

"Find anything?"

Charlotte's thoughts went back to David, holding the map. "A few things," she squeaked.

Angus turned to the conspiracy board. "I've been thinking about our next move in the case. We need to talk to Brian's employer, Lord Farnley."

"Do you think he'll see us?"

Angus considered. "I can't think of any reason why not, but rather than try to book an appointment, I think we should go and see him unannounced. It's always better to retain the element of surprise."

"We should get Grigore to drive us in the Bentley."

Angus put his head on one side. "Why?"

"As he's a toff, he might be more inclined to speak to us if he thinks we have money."

"You have money."

"True," Charlotte conceded.

"All right."

Charlotte's phone beeped a text message alert. She picked it up. It was from David:

Hope you are OK this morning. Wanted to thank you for last night. I'm not sure what else to say – I don't normally do things like this. But I hope to see you again. Not just at your next pottery class. David.

Shit. He was even nice in his texts. Could he get any nicer?

She'd text him back later when Angus was out of the room. David was such a nice man and he had sent her a sweet message. He was handsome, attractive, single, self-deprecating and super nice. With little prospect of anything ever happening with Angus, he was the perfect distraction.

She had slept like a log last night, which was unusual,

but her night with David had tired her out. Her mind ran back to last night's dinner with him. They'd had a delicious meal of pasta and a glass or two of wine, and afterwards they had gone back to his flat above the shop. One thing had quickly led to another.

David had been caring and thoughtful, and had said she could stay the night. However, she'd never been able to sleep well in someone else's bed, so she had left at about midnight after a few more glasses of wine. Grigore had picked her up in the Bentley.

She wasn't sure why – perhaps it was the noir-style detective shows she'd been watching lately – but Charlotte had half expected to see a shrine to his dead wife. She was pleasantly surprised when there was just a small photo of them in the hallway.

There had been a lot of pottery though, and after they'd had sex, Charlotte had inspected a few of the pieces. He was talented, and she'd jokingly told him he should apply to go on *Pottery Throw Down*. He'd laughed, and said that he'd applied but hadn't been selected.

And Grigore, when he picked her up, had been his usual discreet self.

Charlotte replied to David's text when she went to the toilet. There was no way she wanted Angus to know what she'd got up to last night, even by chance.

I'm fine, thanks. It's kind of you to ask.

She'd couldn't add that she didn't normally do things like that either, because although it was a while ago now, she had done that sort of thing a lot before she met Angus. So she added:

I'd like to meet up again soon too. Charlotte.

Chapter Fourteen

Lord Farnley's registered address was Sterling Hall, a mansion a mile away from Liam and Brian's houses and the murder site. The single-track road that led to the house was smooth and well-maintained, unlike the one they'd navigated two days earlier to reach Gary's farm.

Grigore drove them in the Bentley, and as they approached, Angus peered out of the window. The house was a grand brick building, and looked old. Angus guessed at least four hundred years old. Architecture had never been his forte, but three stories with Tudor-style black wooden beams and whitewash on the top floor made him think of several buildings of a similar style in the centre of Exeter. Maybe it was even older than he thought.

Grigore parked right outside the main entrance and opened the door for Charlotte. When she had told him what they were doing and where they were going, Grigore had put on his chauffeur uniform. He always liked to look the part for occasions such as this.

They glanced at the view across the gardens. The house was elevated and the view across the fields was exceptional: green fields as far as the eye could see.

Charlotte sighed. "Places like this always make me want to move to the country."

"Not thought about buying a mansion of your own?" Angus stood beside her, looking at the view.

"I've thought about it, but I'd be lost in a house like this. I'd get lonely very quickly."

They turned to the house. The front door was huge, made of old oak, with carved panels, and black metal fittings. Angus banged the oversized knocker, and immediately the sound of dogs barking in the distance shattered the tranquility of the place. The barking got closer until the dogs were behind the door.

Half a minute later, the door handle moved and the door creaked open a little. "Down, down, you stupid mutts," said a stern female voice.

The dogs continued to bark, and they saw part of a struggle as the woman got herself outside without the dogs coming too.

"Just ignore them," the woman said. She was in her late sixties, wearing a gilet with a cream shirt underneath, an A-line woollen skirt and Ugg boots. Her short grey hair was styled in flicks on either side of her head. "They get excited when we have visitors. Don't get many these days. I'm Lady F. What can I do for you?" Her accent was crisp and posh.

The barking continued behind the door.

"We'd like to speak to Lord Farnley," Angus said.

The woman peered at Angus and Charlotte. Then she looked beyond them to the Bentley and Grigore standing beside it.

"What? Farnley? What about? Who are you?"

"We're private detectives," said Angus. "We're looking into the murder of Brian Letterman.""Private detectives?" She eyed the Bentley again, then stared at Angus. "What sort of private detectives have a Bentley and a chauffeur?"

Angus and Charlotte exchanged glances. "We just need to ask him a few questions. Is he available?"

Lady Farnley put both her hands behind her back and looked up at Angus, who was considerably taller than she was. "What? I suppose so. Usually you'd need an appointment, but he's in the stables and worried about his favourite mare, so a distraction might be in order. She's been very tetchy these last few days. Probably on heat. Her last foal had to be put down. Dreadful situation." She paused. "Come with me," she barked.

She began to walk round the side of the mansion and Angus and Charlotte followed. They saw a stable block made out of the same brick as the main house, with an entrance large enough for carriages to drive in.

Inside the stable block, the temperature dropped and the strong smell of horse manure hit them. When they were used to the dimmer light, they saw a man at the far end, stroking a horse's head. He was about the same age as the woman, and wore a white pinstriped shirt and dark-brown corduroy trousers.

"Bertie dear, these two want to talk to you," the woman he said in a loud voice. "Private Investigators," she added.

The man pulled his gaze away from the horse. "What?"

"I said, these private detectives want to talk to you!" she shouted.

"For God's sake, woman. Can't you send them away and get them to book an appointment?"

"They're not ordinary private detectives. They've got a Bentley and a driver."

Lord Farnley looked Charlotte and Angus up and down. "Oh all right, I have a few minutes. What do you want?"

Lady Farnley walked off without so much as a look at Charlotte and Angus.

Angus went over to the horse and rubbed her nose. "Lovely horse. What's her name?""Clara." Lord Farnley looked at her fondly. "She's been restless lately. The vet says she's on heat, but I'm not sure. She's never been like this before. What do you want to speak to me about, anyway?" Lord Farnley demanded. Politeness, it seemed, was off the menu.

"We're looking into the murder of Brian Letterman. You were his employer, so we'd like to talk to you about him," Angus said.

"Brian? Why are you looking into his murder? They found who did it – it was that Beckett fellow."

Charlotte walked over to the horse and gently stroked the side of her neck. "We've been hired by Mr Beckett to look into the murder. He claims he's innocent."

"Damn stupid thing to waste his money on. A court of law found him guilty. I read the newspaper reports. He was clearly guilty, and a bloody nuisance it was too."

"What do you mean?" Charlotte asked.

"Brian was a damn fine employee. He was gamekeeper, but he also helped manage the livestock. I haven't found anyone with his knowledge or experience since. Not here, anyway. Everyone who applied for the job is either too young or wants a golden hello payment. Bloody cheek."

"Can you tell us anything about Brian and how he got on with the staff here?" Angus asked.

Lord Farnley frowned. "Not much to say. He reported directly to me, and he was exceptional. He wasn't one of those men who larked around. He always kept his head down and got on with it. If I could wring Beckett's neck for murdering my best employee, I would."

"I'm so sorry you haven't been able to replace him," Charlotte said, and tilted her head slightly. Angus knew that head tilt. She did it when she was trying to calm someone down, and she did it on purpose.

"Advertised the job, as I said, but only half-wits have applied."

"I'm sorry to hear that," said Angus, and cleared his throat. "Was Brian particularly friendly with anyone here?"

Lord Farnley thought for a moment. "Only Meg."

"Meg?"

"The dog!" Lord Farnley roared with laughter, then his face went red and he had a coughing fit. Eventually, he calmed down. "As I said, he kept himself to himself and worked hard. Now, I don't understand how Beckett has the barefaced cheek to try and get himself off the hook, but I can't tell you anything else. It was a working relationship: we didn't socialise. Nothing like that."

"He didn't drop comments about himself or his life at all?"

"What? No. Look, I'm sorry I can't help more but I was his employer, not his friend. If you want to know more about him, you'll have to talk to his family and friends."

"Thank you for talking to us. One more thing: I want to have a look around Brian's house."

"What? No. Why would you want to have a snoop around? Police went over it with all their forensics and such so there's nothing you'd find there that they didn't." Lord Farnley turned back to his horse.

As they walked back to the car, Charlotte turned to Angus. "You stroked that horse as if you know about them."

"I do, a bit. My daughter Grace was mad about horses. She had her own for a few years, and I used to help her at the stables when I could."

Charlotte smiled. "Well, you're a bit of a dark horse. Pun intended."

Angus smiled back and shook his head. "Horses are ridiculously expensive. Grace's horse was a money pit. Still, it kept her happy."

"I read somewhere that if you buy your daughter a horse, they get so absorbed by them that it delays their interest in boys by five years. Is that true?"

Angus considered for a moment. "Yeah, I think it probably was money well spent."

When they got back to the car they found Grigore and Lady Farnley standing beside it, talking. The dogs who had been so noisy when they'd arrived, and who turned out to be two Dalmatians, were there too. One was running around on the grass nearby, and the other was sitting at Grigore's feet, presumably waiting for a treat.

"Damn nice car you've got there," Lady Farnley said as they approached.

"Thank you," Charlotte said.

"My father gave me a Bentley for my eighteenth birthday. Didn't get a driver with it, though. I crashed it a couple of years later and it had to be scrapped. Horrible mess it made of the tree. That had to be scrapped too. He never stopped going on about it. The tree, not the car."

"I hope you weren't hurt," Angus said.

"What? No. Only had a bit of whiplash. Bentleys are built like tanks. Bit more comfortable than tanks, though. Did you get what you needed?"

"Yes. Thanks for taking us Lord Farnley."

Lady Farnley called out to the dog on the grass, which was currently urinating, "Come on, Meg." The dog ran over and she walked off without saying goodbye.

Chapter Fifteen

When Angus had gone for the day, Charlotte took out her phone and reread the message David had left her that morning. They hadn't talked about meeting up again last night, and he hadn't mentioned anything specific in the text. She'd see him again at the pottery class next week and she examined her feelings about whether or not she wanted to see him again.

Her house was quiet, and she had no plans for the evening.

It took her one minute to text David: *You free tonight?*

He texted back five minutes later. *Yes. Want to meet up?*

She replied: *I thought you'd never ask. I'll bring food.*

When Angus got home, he went for a run again. He was still a little tired from the run the day before, but he always felt better after running two days in a row. It would help clear his head, too, which was full of the case. He had always believed he was a good judge of character, and he went over the conversation he'd had with Liam when he'd agreed to take on the case.

Liam had been stressed. That was understandable: prison wasn't an easy ride. It could have been because Liam didn't like the fact that he'd been caught, but Angus's gut feeling told him over and over again that it was because Liam was innocent. He couldn't put it down to anything concrete, which was annoying. But time and again he'd learnt to trust his gut instinct, some would call it guesswork, but it was more than that. If he was spiritual, he'd put the feeling down to some higher power guiding him.

So far, they hadn't discovered anything beyond the police investigation. Woody had been as thorough as Angus knew he would. He had to look beyond that.

He wondered if there was anything hidden on Brian's laptop. A report into its contents was part of the evidence from the investigation, but the contents had not been disclosed in court. Therefore he couldn't be sure there wasn't anything on there of interest.

The laptop had been handed back to Brian's daughter after Liam's conviction. He made a mental note to ask if Jessica would let him see it. She might not even have it any more, but if you didn't ask, the answer was always no.

Just after he got out of the shower, towel around his waist and hair dripping, his phone rang. He looked at the display: a blocked number. He pressed Answer. "Angus Darrow."

There was silence on the line. "Hello?" Angus said.

There was a rustling sound. "H-hello. Are you the detective?" It was a man's voice, and Angus quickly guessed they were below forty. There was the faint sound of people chatting in the background's if the caller was in a public place.

"Yes. How can I help?"

"You need to know something. Something about Brian."

Angus's heart started to race. "Who is this?" He made sure his voice was enquiring but not accusatory.

"I-I can't say. Oh God, they'll kill me if they find out I've talked to you."

"They won't find out. Tell me what you know."

There was another long pause. "I – I know Liam didn't kill Brian. He was set up."

"You're sure? How do you know?"

"Someone else killed Brian because...because he found out about...about..."

"Who killed him? What did he find out about?"

"I can't say, but— Shit..." There was a rustling sound and the line went dead.

Angus looked at his phone. The call had ended. He went straight downstairs, found his notebook and wrote down everything the man had said.

Then he phoned Charlotte. It went straight to voice-mail: "Hi, this is Charlotte. I'm avoiding someone I don't like. Leave a message, and if I don't call back, it's you."

Angus had to suppress a laugh despite his annoyance at her not answering. Usually, if he called and she couldn't answer, she'd call back thirty seconds later, so he never left a message. This time, he decided to talk.

"It's Angus. It's getting late, so we'll talk in the morning, but something interesting has happened with the case. See you tomorrow."

He got dressed and went downstairs to make something to eat, and was halfway through cooking when he realised that Charlotte still hadn't called him back. That was unusual. Even more unusual was that by the time he went to bed a few hours later, there was still no call from her.

For a moment he wondered whether Charlotte was OK. Then he decided that it was stupid to chase her. She was a grown woman. If she wasn't answering her phone, it was because she was busy doing something else.

Charlotte took the now lukewarm Indian takeaway out of the bag. The popadoms were crushed: she'd put the bag down in a hurry as David kissed her. She had hardly got in the door before they began ripping each other's clothes off.

His kitchen was small, but clean and cosy. "Have you got a microwave?" she asked. "I think it's salvageable." She took the lid off a foil container and tipped the curry onto a plate.

"It's over there." David pointed to the microwave in the corner.

Charlotte put the plate inside and switched it on. "Next time we'll order afterwards." She turned to him and smiled.

David tipped the contents of the second container onto a plate. "That sounds promising: next time!"

Charlotte laughed. "Am I being presumptuous?"

"Not at all. But you bought me coffee and dinner yesterday and a takeaway tonight. It's my turn to buy dinner next time. You'll be broke by the end of the month."

Charlotte thought about her latest bank balance. If the end of the month was in several hundred years' time, then that might be true. She hadn't told David about her financial situation. Should she? People didn't normally go around telling others how much money they had unless they were attention-seeking tossers. How would she approach it, anyway? And how would he react? She didn't know him well enough to judge.

Instead, she simply said, "OK, you can buy next time."

David raised his eyebrows and smiled. "Tomorrow?"
She smiled back. "Sounds good."

Chapter Sixteen

The next morning, Angus arrived at the usual time. Charlotte wasn't long out of the shower: her hair was still wet. She was dressed in dark-grey track-suit bottoms and a black vest top. Angus couldn't help appreciating how effortlessly beautiful she looked, despite being dressed down.

Their morning routine had become familiar: coffee, then a discussion of the case in hand. This time they were in the lounge. Charlotte sat cross-legged on the Chesterfield, hugging a cushion.

"I'm sorry I didn't call you back last night," she said. "I got your message, but by the time I saw it, it was eleven o'clock and I didn't want to wake you. What's the news?"

Angus told her about the phone call and read out what the man had said from his notebook.

"And the call ended suddenly?"

Angus put his notebook on the arm of the chair. "Yep. There was rustling in the background, then the line went dead."

"That doesn't bode well. And it was definitely a blocked number?"

"It was. Is there any way to find out the number?"

Charlotte raked her hand through her wet hair. "Your phone company will be able to look at the computer records for the call and get the number, even though it was blocked. But they won't give you the number: that's the whole point of call blocking. The police can ask, though. Do you have an ex-colleague you could contact to request it?"

Angus winced. "There's no way your brother would do it, and I'd need a good reason. There are a couple of people I could ask, but to be honest, I don't think they'll do it either. It would be a big favour, and if their superior officers found out they'd be in big trouble."

"I could hack the telecoms company. Which one is it?" She raised her eyebrows hopefully.

Angus shook his head. "No. That's not an option." He was sure that hacking a telecoms company would be easy for her, but no. They had to do things by the book.

Charlotte sighed. "Which company is it? I'll see if I can get a friend of a friend to find out for us."

Angus told her, and Charlotte disappeared into her office. Ten minutes later, she came into the lounge, phone held to her ear. "That's brilliant, thanks. I'll WhatsApp the number it went to and the date and time. Thanks so much, you're a star. I'll transfer the money as soon as you're done."

She ended the call and clapped her hands. "Turns out one of my old staff works at your provider as their head of cybersecurity. He's going to get the number for me."

"That's great. How much is that costing you?"

"What? Oh, not much. Everyone has a price, remember. His is quite low." Charlotte smiled.

It wasn't long before Charlotte's phone rang. She took

Angus's notepad and wrote down a phone number. Not only that, but a name too.

"Thanks, you're a hero. I'll transfer the money now." Charlotte ended the call and held up the notebook. "Darren Gilford. Apparently he lives in the village next to Liam and Brian."

Angus stared at the notepad. "I don't remember his name being in any of the reports."

Charlotte shook her head. "Me neither. I'll just transfer that money and then we can start finding out who he is."

They went into the study and Charlotte began an internet search on Darren. "Oh, hello. This is interesting!" she said, a few minutes later. "Darren not only lives in the next village, but he works for Lord Farnley too."

"That *is* interesting." Angus moved round to Charlotte's side of the desk to read the screen. "He works as a game-keeper, like Brian did."

Charlotte spun her chair to face Angus. "I wonder why he hasn't called you again."

"He sounded scared. My guess is that he was inter-rupted when he was on the phone to me."

"What should we do? Should we phone him?"

"No. We need to go and see him."

Charlotte looked at her watch. "When?"

"Tonight. After work, assuming he works normal hours. Although I'd guess that a gamekeeper might have evening work, especially in the summer with the long days. I think we should go when it's dark. He sounded scared, and we don't know who he's scared of."

"Tonight?" Charlotte repeated, remembering her rendezvous with David that evening, when he would buy her dinner. She'd have to postpone it. "Er, OK. Yes, that's fine. I'll check when the sun is due to set." She tapped at the keyboard. "It'll be pitch black by 9.45 pm."

"All right, we'll get there just before, then. By the way, can you check through the report for information on Brian's laptop? See if there's anything interesting mentioned."

Charlotte nodded. "I did check, and nothing seemed interesting or relevant, but I'll take another look. His daughter has it now, doesn't she?"

"Apparently it was released to her once they'd got all the data off."

"She might still have it, but chances are she's either got rid of it or she's using it herself. I don't think she'll be open to letting us go over it."

Angus walked over to the conspiracy board and stared at the photo of Jessica. "You may be right, but we can try."

Charlotte leaned back in her chair. "I could hack her Wi-Fi and find out if the laptop's there."

Angus turned around and gave her a look. Charlotte shrugged.

"Have a closer look at the laptop report," he said.

Charlotte rolled her eyes. "I'll do that now."

Half an hour later, she'd gone through the report with a fine-tooth comb. She sighed. "There's nothing relevant except for a few emails that Brian sent to the police about Liam. Nothing in his internet search history except the local takeaway opening times and the local council planning department."

Angus looked up from the report he was reading. "What did he look at on the planning website?"

Charlotte picked up the report. "It says here that he looked at a list of recent planning applications."

"He didn't look at any of the applications?"

"Nope."

"And he didn't look at any other websites?"

"Suspiciously, no. But I suppose not everyone uses the internet or computers as much as I do."

Angus turned back to the conspiracy board for a moment. "Was there anything about his phone? You know, websites he'd visited?"

Charlotte leafed through the report. "There was no website history on the phone. He hardly had any apps installed either. So strange."

Angus smiled. "Only strange to you."

Chapter Seventeen

Angus looked at the car clock: it was 9.37pm. They were in his VW Golf, in front of them the sky was gentle pink and fiery red which cast long shadows. It was a warm glow that gave an enchanting tranquillity.

Behind them was dark.

He'd parked around the corner from Darren's house and they were waiting a few minutes until it got even darker.

He turned to look at Charlotte. She was gazing at her phone, scrolling through something. He didn't look to see what she was reading. She'd been remarkably good lately about not being able to hack everyone and everything. However, he couldn't help wondering whether, at some point, he would have to ask her to hack something, despite his insistence that she didn't do it.

Charlotte put her phone in her bag. "Shall we go?"

"Yes."

Darren's house was one of four terraced houses, all rendered and painted white, with large front gardens. Evergreen bushes surrounded the house, and a truck with an open back sat on the drive.

Angus rang the doorbell. He half-expected the sound of barking to break out again, as he assumed a gamekeeper would keep dogs.

A woman opened the door a moment later. She was slim, in her early thirties, with blonde hair in a ponytail, wearing jeans and a white T-shirt. "Can I help?" Her eyes darted from Angus to Charlotte.

"Is Darren in?" Angus said.

"Who are you?"

"We'd just like a quick word." Angus gave her a reassuring smile.

"All right. But if you're selling something, we're not interested."

"We're not selling anything."

She closed the door. Thirty seconds later, a man in this thirties, messy blond hair and unshaven for a few days opened it. "Yeah?"

"Darren Gilford?"

"Yeah, who are you?"

Angus could see the woman they'd spoken to nearby, eavesdropping. He lowered his voice. "I'm Angus Darrow. You called me yesterday."

Darren's eyes widened and he gabbled, "Dunno who you are, but I didn't call you."

"I recognise your voice."

Darren came outside and pulled the door to behind him. "Look, I don't know what you think you heard, or who called you, but it wasn't me, all right? So piss off." He went into the house and slammed the door.

"It was definitely him," Charlotte said. "The look on his face when you told him who you were said it all."

Angus sighed. "Yes, it was him."

"What do we do now?"

Angus took out his phone. "I'm going to call him."

He pressed some buttons and waited for the call to connect. Then he took the phone from his ear. "Straight to voicemail." He waited for the message to end, then spoke. "Darren, we need to talk. Call me again. Whatever you wanted to say, you can tell me in confidence. I haven't told anyone that you called me."

He ended the call and turned to Charlotte. "We'll come back, but in the morning."

The next morning, Angus set off on his own to visit Darren. He hadn't told Charlotte: he had decided on the spur of the moment, after he got dressed. To get Darren to talk, it was best to be as discreet as possible.

He went to Darren's house first. As he had expected, the truck had gone from the driveway. He drove in the direction of Lord Farnley's house. He wasn't sure where on the large estate Darren might be, but he had to try and find him.

Angus found himself on the long road leading to the mansion house, and spotted Darren's truck parked off-road about halfway up on the left-hand side, near a wooded area. He didn't want to risk his car getting stuck off-road, so he parked at the nearest passing place, got out, and walked to the truck.

It was locked, and there was no sign of Darren inside. The open cargo bed contained a folded tarpaulin and nothing else.

Angus surveyed the landscape. Darren had most likely gone into the woods. The ground was still damp from last night's rain, and looked boggy. He looked down at his smart black shoes. Luckily, he kept a spare pair of trainers in his car boot for situations like this. Angus returned to his car, changed into the trainers and walked into the woods to find Darren.

There was a natural path between the trees, worn by walkers, and Angus followed it. The only sound apart from his footsteps was birds chirping. Whatever Darren was doing, it was further in the woods.

Angus kept walking, the path becoming less defined and more uneven. Then, at a break in the trees ahead, he glimpsed a splash of orange. Angus quickened his pace, and as he got closer the clothing became a person. A person stretched out on the floor.

Angus ran towards the person.

It was Darren.

He only had to take one look to know that he was dead.

Darren lay with his face to the side, and his eyes wide open.

Angus moved closer to body and felt for a pulse on his neck. Just as he suspected, there was nothing, but his body was still warm. He'd clearly only been dead a short time. On the side of his head was a wound that looked like a blunt blow. Angus looked around to check whoever had done this, wasn't still around. He didn't want to be the next victim.

A tree branch thick, about a foot long with a blood stain lay next to Darren.

Satisfying himself that there was no-one near, he dialled 999.

It took the police twenty minutes to get to the site. Angus had used the What3Words app to give them his location. That app was proving to be very useful.

He knew what Charlotte would say if he complimented

the app: there was a world of useful tech out there and if he wasn't such a technophobe he could benefit from it. She was right, of course, but he liked being a technophobe. It kept life simple. Several of his friends were obsessed with social media; one was constantly on Tinder and similar apps, looking for a date. He'd never do that: online dating was a no-no. Besides, he was still hoping that at some point, he and Charlotte would become romantically involved.

Uniformed officers arrived first. They called through to the station, then asked Angus to stand aside while they cordoned off the area.

Shortly afterwards, a pair of plain-clothes detectives arrived and examined the scene. Then they eyed Angus, who was waiting nearby. He knew the drill: he'd done exactly the same a few times over the years.

While he watched them, he texted Charlotte.

I went out this morning to talk to Darren at work. He's been murdered.

She texted back a moment later.

What? Oh God, how awful. Why did you go without me?

He didn't have time to reply. One of the detectives approached him. He was in his mid-forties, wearing skinny black jeans and a dark denim shirt. "I'm DCI Peter Spencer. You found the body, did you, sir?"

"I did."

"And your name is Angus Darrow?" He looked at his notebook.

"Yes."

"I'd like you to come down to the station to help us with our enquiries."

"Er, OK."

Chapter Eighteen

Charlotte texted Angus again: *Call me when you're free.*

He still hadn't answered. That wasn't completely unknown, but he never usually left it this long.

She felt hurt and annoyed. Firstly, because he'd gone to see Darren on his own, and more importantly, she'd missed out on the action. She felt bad that Darren was dead and maybe they should have done things differently, but it meant that the case was hotting up. In the circumstances, Angus's lack of communication was disappointing.

There was nothing else for it: she'd have to activate the secret location app she'd put on his phone. She hadn't used it for a while, as she knew that tracking Angus's location was a bit too close to stalking, but she did worry about him. He was a single man, with no one except her to worry over where or how he was.

She tapped the screen to locate him and drummed her fingers on the table while she waited.

The map loaded. It showed a pin that Angus was in

Okehampton. She zoomed in. Okehampton Police Station. She frowned. "What are you doing there, Angus?"

Charlotte pictured a few scenarios. Visiting a former work colleague? Asking for help with the case? Helping the police with their enquiries? That one didn't sound good.

She decided to call him again. The phone rang, but Angus didn't answer and it went to voicemail.

Unlike her, Angus hadn't recorded a personal voicemail message: his was the standard automated one. She'd have to persuade him to record one, because she wanted to hear his voice even if it was a recording.

Charlotte phoned Grigore and he answered straight away. "I need you to drive me to Okehampton."

Half an hour later, Charlotte checked the app again. Angus was still at the police station. Grigore pulled up outside the station a couple of minutes later. It was at the end of the high street, an old Victorian building, and if it wasn't for the modern police cars parked outside, Charlotte would have felt as if she'd stepped back in time. She walked to the front door and went in.

A long corridor lined with noticeboards led to a hatch at the end. Charlotte glanced at the boards as she passed. Some held wanted posters, some displayed general information for the public, warning them to be scam aware or reminding them not to use their mobile phone while driving.

She approached the hatch and peered in. On the other side was a small office with two desks. On the desks were computers, the screens placed sideways to the hatch so that she couldn't read them. She pressed the buzzer for help and a moment later, a police officer appeared. He was young and slim, perhaps in his mid-twenties, with brown hair. "Can I help?"

Charlotte looked him in the eye. "Hello. I'm looking for my colleague, Angus Darrow. I believe he's here?"

The officer looked to his right. Charlotte couldn't see what he was looking at. "Er, hold on a minute, I'll check."

He disappeared and she heard a door open and close. She drummed her fingers on the ledge of the hatch as she waited.

Eventually he came back. "Mr Darrow has been helping us with the investigation. We're just waiting for a lawyer."

Charlotte laughed in surprise. "What? Why would he need a lawyer if he's helping you? Unless you suspect him. Don't be silly! Is this his idea of a joke?"

The officer's expression changed from apologetic to serious. "This is not a joke, madam."

Charlotte blinked twice. "You're serious?"

"I am, madam."

"Oh my God, what fresh hell is this?" She put the palm of her hand on her forehead. "Shit, shit, shit."

Now was not the time to panic, but it was hard to resist. She should call her brother Mark – he'd sort it out. Maybe Angus had called Mark already. Maybe Mark wouldn't help, because he was angry that they were looking into one of his cases.

No, a lawyer. Phone her lawyer, that's what she needed to do first.

The officer's voice broke through her panicked thoughts. "Are you all right, madam?"

She lowered her hand and turned to him. "If you think Angus has anything to do with a murder, you're nuts. It's the most ridiculous thing I've ever heard. He's the last man on earth who'd kill someone. He's the kindest, most law-abiding, sweet-hearted man I've ever met. You do realise he's an ex-police detective?"

"We are aware of that, madam," he said, in a patronising tone. "That doesn't mean that he's above suspicion." He paused. "Are you close?" One of his eyebrows lifted as he said 'close'.

Charlotte knew exactly what he was implying and she didn't mind at all. "Yes, we're close. *Very* close. I want to see him."

"I'm sorry, but you can't."

"For God's sake, why not?"

"It's not allowed until he's been interviewed."

Charlotte put her hands on the hatch shelf, bowed her head and closed her eyes. If she wasn't careful she would shout at the officer, and that would only get her arrested too. Or even worse, removed from the station.

She had to think fast and direct her anger towards helping him.

Chapter Nineteen

Angus sat opposite DCI Spencer in one of the interview rooms. A female police officer came into the room with a coffee in a polystyrene cup and put it in front of Angus. He eyed it, knowing it would be lukewarm. That was deliberate, in case a prisoner decided to throw it over a police officer.

"You'd think that polystyrene cups would have been banned by now as bad for the environment," Angus found himself saying.

The WPC looked at him as she sat down beside DCI Spencer. "It's a precaution, sir, to make sure you don't scald yourself." Angus knew that too, but he didn't say anything. The sooner this was over with, the better.

Sitting next to him was his brief, a local lawyer provided free of charge by the government. He'd spoken to Angus alone beforehand, and Angus had the impression that despite his advancing years, the lawyer had no experience with murder cases.

The female officer pressed the record button on the video, then stated the date, the time and who was there.

DCI Spencer leaned forward. "First of all, Mr Darrow, you're not under arrest, and you can leave at any time. I'd like you to explain in your own words what happened this morning. Start from when you got up."

Angus raised an eyebrow. He wouldn't have started with that. He'd have asked about his relationship with the victim, if any. "I got up, left my house at 7.15am, and went to Darren's house. When I discovered he wasn't at home, I drove to Lord Farnley's estate. I saw Darren's truck parked at the side of the road leading to the house. I parked my car, changed into trainers and went to find him in the woods. I found him dead and I phoned you." It was factual and all the information he needed.

DCI Spencer took notes as Angus spoke and stopped writing when he'd finished then looked up, his eyes narrowed assessing Angus. "Why did you change your shoes?"

"It was muddy. I didn't want to get my shoes dirty."

Angus read the officer's handwriting upside down. He'd written 'Dirty shoes'.

"Can you explain why you went to see Darren so early in the morning?"

"He'd called me the day before, saying he had information about who really killed Brian Letterman, and I wanted to talk to him about it."

DCI Spencer stared at Angus. "What has that murder got to do with you?"

"I'm a private detective. I was hired by Liam Beckett to prove his innocence."

"And what did Darren tell you?"

"He didn't. When I visited him last night, he denied ever calling me."

"You visited him last night?" Spencer leaned forward, a glint in his eye as though he'd caught a fox in the henhouse.

"I did, but he wouldn't speak to me." He almost mentioned that Charlotte had been with him, then decided not to. If they thought he'd murdered Darren, there was no reason to drag her into this.

Spencer studied him. "You're a private detective?"

"Yes."

"And, I see from your record, an ex-police officer."

"Yes."

Spencer stared at him.

The door opened and an officer poked his head in. "Sir, can I have a word?"

Spencer sighed, went outside, and returned a moment later. "Mr Darrow, it appears that your girlfriend has sent her lawyer over. He's outside, ready to represent you, but you have to give permission." He handed Angus a business card.

Girlfriend? thought Angus. It could only be Charlotte. How did she know he was here? He looked at the card. *Hugo Cavendish, Kensington Crescent, London, SW 3.* He recognised the name Hugo: he'd heard her mention it on the phone before.

He looked at the lawyer sitting beside him. "If you'd prefer your girlfriend's lawyer, that's your choice." He sounded relieved.

Angus hesitated. He didn't want to take something from Charlotte. Hugo Cavendish would be expensive: Kensington was one of the most expensive parts of London. Then he eyed the lawyer beside him. Was he really going to turn down a top lawyer out of pride? "Thanks, I'll take Mr Cavendish."

The other lawyer left the room and Hugo Cavendish

came in. He wore a Savile Row three-piece suit in navy pinstripe, with a red polka-dot handkerchief in his top pocket. He was at least sixty, with grey hair and pleasant features. Angus stood up and shook his hand.

"Hugo Cavendish," the lawyer announced in a voice of crisp consonants and rounded vowels, resonating a posh English accent. He smiled at Angus, and put his briefcase on the table. "My client won't be answering any more of your questions. You must release him now."

Spencer stood up and faced Hugo. "I need him to explain why he was following the murder victim and how he just happened to find him dead."

Hugo replied crisply. "You need evidence that he committed the crime, and you have none. If you would like to show me exactly why you suspect him..."

Spencer frowned.

"Exactly. Mr Darrow, we're leaving."

Outside the police station, Charlotte threw herself at Angus. "I thought they were going to charge you with murder!" she cried, burying her head in his chest. Angus couldn't help wrapping his arms around her. She held on for a long time, then pulled away and put her hands on her hips. "I'm still really annoyed that you went without me."

Angus's euphoria at the hug disappeared instantly. "So that we could both be accused of murdering Darren?"

"They wouldn't have been so suspicious if there had been two of us, and everyone knows the stats on men vs women murderers. Men commit 80% of all murders."

Angus pushed his glasses up his nose. She was right: and murderers rarely travelled in pairs. He was tired and hungry, and decided not to argue. "Can we go and get something to eat?"

Charlotte nodded. "I saw a cafe round the corner. Let's go there. Then you can promise not to leave me out of the action again."

The cafe was like a Tardis: the tiny entrance opened into a huge space. They were greeted by the warm aroma of freshly brewed coffee and jazz music in the background. The interior was dated but well-kept, with a cosy, inviting atmosphere.

They ordered at the counter, then went to a table. Angus took his glasses off and rubbed his eyes.

"You look very different without those," Charlotte commented.

Angus shrugged. "Necessary evil. I wore contact lenses for years, but in the end my eyes rejected them. Even the really expensive ones."

Charlotte put her elbow on the table and rested her chin on her hand. "So, tell me everything."

Angus put his glasses back on. "I went to Darren's house this morning. His truck had gone, so I drove to Lord Farnley's estate. Halfway up the lane to the house, I saw Darren's truck parked on the verge. I went into the wooded area beyond and found him dead."

"Just terrible." Charlotte frowned, then sat back.

Their coffees arrived and Angus took a long sip. His questioning had been inconvenient, but at least he was free now. His stomach rumbled and the aroma of food cooking wasn't helping to quell his hunger. "How did you get your lawyer to me so quickly?" he asked.

"Helicopter."

Angus put his head in his hands. "Jesus. How much did that cost? Not to mention the lawyer."

Charlotte pursed her lips. "Not as much as I thought it would." She leaned forward, prised one of his hands away from his head, and held it. "I couldn't just sit back and let them implicate you with a murder you didn't commit. That's what they were trying to do wasn't it? Remember, I need this job."

"You know I'll never be able to repay you?"

"You already have. I don't need repayment in money, I need it in work. Work with you. Which is why I'm so annoyed that you went without me."

Angus took a deep breath. "All right."

Charlotte grinned. "Excellent. Just leave everything up to Hugo. He never loses."

"They don't have anything on me," Angus replied. "They just found it suspicious that I visited him last night and then this morning, in the middle of nowhere, found him dead. If I was in the DCI's position, I'd be looking into me, too."

"Hugo mentioned something about your trainers. What was that about?"

Angus took another sip of coffee, then shook his head and smiled. "I didn't want to get my shoes dirty when I went into the woods to look for Darren, so I swapped to my trainers. DCI Spencer thought I was hiding any potential footprints."

"That's ridiculous. Why would you swap your shoes and then call the police?"

"I know. I don't think he's dealt with many murder cases before."

They were interrupted by the arrival of the food. Angus had ordered a full English breakfast. A plate of sausages, bacon, hash browns, baked beans, black pudding, mushrooms, tomatoes and two poached eggs on toast was the perfect remedy for the stress of the last few hours.

He looked at the empty space in front of Charlotte. "Are you sure you won't have something to eat?"

"I'm too stressed." She took a sip of coffee. "More caffeine probably won't help, but it's that or wine."

Angus tucked into his food, and silence fell.

"So, what next?" Charlotte asked eventually. "With the case, I mean."

"Someone killed Darren because he knew who really killed Brian. They wanted to shut him up."

"It was definitely murder, then?"

"Yep. Hit over the head with a blunt object. We need to talk to his partner."

"Don't you think we should leave it a few days?" said Charlotte. "Darren was only murdered this morning. She'll still be in shock."

Angus considered this. "I think we should go straight round. There may well be a FLO – a family liaison officer – there with her, and they may not let us in, but we have to try. She might know something which helps us to discover what his movements were this morning. Or maybe she could tell us if anyone had contacted him recently."

"I'll get Grigore to drive us," said Charlotte.

"I need to collect my car from the police station, too," said Angus. "They took it this morning to go through it for evidence."

Charlotte snorted. "That will have been a dead end. Your car's always pristine."

"Nothing wrong with having a clean car, inside and out."

The door of the cafe opened and they looked over. In walked Charlotte's brother, Mark 'Woody' Lockwood.

Charlotte stood up and hugged him. He bear-hugged her back, lifting her off the floor. "All right, Charlie."

"No, I'm not all right."

Woody let go of her, pulled out the chair next to Angus and sat down. He extended his hand to Angus, who shook it briefly.

"What took you so long?" Charlotte scolded.

Woody held up his hands in mock surrender. "Hey, enough of the aggro. I get enough of that at work."

"I phoned you hours ago. Angus was kept in a cell for hours, accused of murder. You could have stopped all of it."

Woody shook his head. "Easy, tiger. I was busy. I can't tell you what I was doing, but it was important. And no, I couldn't stop them questioning Angus. That would be interfering with a case, and I'd be up on a disciplinary pretty damn quick."

Charlotte narrowed her eyes. "Have you spoken to that idiot who arrested him?"

"I have, and he knows he's got zero evidence of Angus murdering this man."

"Of course he hasn't any evidence, because Angus didn't do it. Stupid bloody excuse for a police officer. I might get Hugo to sue him for something."

"Got Hugo in, did ya?" Woody looked from Charlotte to Angus, who was still eating his all-day breakfast. "Charlie, you do realise that Angus is a big boy who can look after himself?"

Charlotte tensed. "Of course I bloody well do!" The owner of the cafe looked over, frowning.

She lowered her voice. "Of course I do. But I wasn't going to let them charge him. We both know that Angus is the last man on earth who'd murder someone, and there's no way some two-bit small-town lawyer would know anything close to Hugo when it comes to something like this. Angus deserves the best lawyer, and that's Hugo."

"Angus would have made them realise pretty quickly that he was innocent," said Woody. "They had nothing to go on, anyway. Just the fact that he'd found the body."

Angus put his knife and fork down. "I am still here, you know."

Woody raised his eyebrows at Charlotte in a 'told you so' way.

Angus picked up his cutlery. "I don't want you to sue the police."

Charlotte stared at him. "Why?"

"Because I don't want you to. Woody, what can you tell us about the murder?"

"Not much. Just that Darren Gilford died from being struck by a blunt object, probably a tree branch they found next to him about at least half an hour before you found him."

Angus whistled. "That's pretty close. No wonder they arrested me." He ate another mouthful of food.

"So, who was nearby half an hour before you turned up, Angus?" Charlotte asked. "That's what we need to know."

"They're going to look for mobile-phone tracking evidence," said Woody. "That might help."

"Anyone with knowledge of technology would leave their phone at home, though," Charlotte replied.

Woody nodded. "Unless the murder was committed on impulse. Very often it is." Woody picked up the menu on the table and scanned it. "Since you've dragged me all this way, Charlie, the very least you can do is get me a coffee and something to eat. I'll have what Angus is demolishing."

Charlotte nodded and went to the counter.

Woody turned to Angus the moment she'd gone. "I'm

sorry I didn't get there sooner. I phoned the Deputy Chief Constable as soon as I heard, and he put pressure on DCI Spencer."

Angus nodded as he loaded his fork with the last of his meal. "It was inconvenient, but no real harm done."

"I'd have been spitting fire if it had been me."

Angus smiled, "I don't doubt it."

"Why were you looking into this Darren guy?"

Angus ate his last mouthful and put his knife and fork together. "He phoned me yesterday from a blocked number. He told me that he knew who'd really killed Brian."

Woody looked at Charlotte, standing by the counter. "And I'm guessing that somehow my little sister found out the blocked number."

"She did. We went to see him last night but he denied phoning me. It was him, though. I recognised his voice. He was scared, very scared, and sent us away. That's why I went back this morning, to see if he would open up."

"I don't remember him from the original investigation."

"He wasn't in it. We checked."

"Did you think he was bullshitting?"

"Who was bullshitting?" Charlotte had returned to the table.

"We're talking about Darren," said Angus.

Woody frowned. "Tell me about him."

"He worked as a gamekeeper at Lord Farnley's estate. Brian worked there too, and now they're both dead." Angus drained his cup.

Woody sighed and shut his eyes for a moment, then turned to Angus. "All right, let's suppose for a moment that Liam is innocent and Darren was murdered because he knew something. Who do you think might have something to hide that Brian and Darren would both know?"

Angus shook his head. "No idea, but I want to talk to his partner. She might know something."

Woody nodded and sat back. "I thought you were barking up the wrong tree when you took this case on, but I'm starting to think that you might be on to something. If you are, I'm going to look like a right idiot."

Chapter Twenty

Angus left Charlotte and Woody not long afterwards. He wanted to get home and wash the experience away under a hot shower. But when he pulled up on his drive, he suddenly realised that he needed to go for a run and clear his head.

While he had remained calm both in the cell and in the interview, Angus was annoyed. Really annoyed, and stressed. He hadn't been this stressed since Charlotte had been kidnapped. He rested his head on the steering wheel and took a deep breath. He ought to take that class on meditation for beginners that he'd seen advertised in the corner shop. One of his friends had mentioned that they'd started meditating a while ago and it had helped with all sorts of things.

He was grateful to Charlotte for getting her lawyer, though. He hadn't thanked her enough before leaving the cafe, but he'd do it properly the next time he saw her. Maybe take her some flowers, like Ross had not so long ago.

That made him realise that he still hadn't worked out a gift for her birthday. He owed her a lot. Too much.

Angus pulled himself together and got out of the car. Sitting in his car moping wouldn't help. He'd go for a run, then spend half an hour in the shower.

He let himself in, picked up the post on the mat and looked through it. It was mostly junk mail, apart from a bank statement and a blank envelope. He opened it and pulled out a single A4 piece of paper. On it were a few lines of printed computer text:

Stop sticking your nose into Brian's death. Liam did it, he's playing you for fools.

Angus turned the paper over, but the other side was blank. There was nothing else inside the envelope either. He took a photo of it with his phone and sent it to Charlotte on WhatsApp.

She replied quickly: *WTF??!!!*

A moment later, she called. "Is that real?"

"Why would it not be real?" Angus walked upstairs and went into his bedroom.

Charlotte sighed. "Of course I know it's real. It was a rhetorical question. Anyway, was it hand delivered or mailed?"

"Hand delivered."

"You'd better step up your security. If someone is sending you poison-pen letters, who knows what they'll do next?"

"No, I won't. They're just trying to frighten us and I won't be cowed."

There was silence at the other end of the phone.

"And I don't need you to do anything either," Angus added. "Don't even think about it."

"But—"

"No buts. I'm going for a run. We'll talk more tomorrow." And without waiting for an answer, he ended the call.

Two hours later, and Charlotte arrived at her second pottery class. She was the last to arrive, and when she stepped in, David was stood talking to the others in the class, cup of tea in hand. Maggie and Dennis were there again, Dennis stood awkwardly to the side of the others, and Maggie stood next to David. There was also a new student, a man in his seventies, slim, grey hair dressed in jeans and a t-shirt.

David gave her a warm smile as she approached, and introduced her to a new student. "Good evening Charlotte. This is Paul. He'll be joining us for the remainder of the lessons."

"Hi," Charlotte said to Paul. She smiled at David, and they exchanged a knowing look.

"Tea?" David asked.

"Yes please."

He disappeared into the kitchen, and Charlotte turned to Paul. "Have you done this before?"

"When I was young." Paul said. "These lessons were a birthday present from my daughter, I'm looking forward to it. I'm such a fan of *Pottery Throw Down* on TV."

"I am too!" Charlotte said.

David returned with Charlotte's tea as Charlotte and Paul chatted. Then David got everyone's attention. "Right, so today you're going to attempt a small pot on the pottery wheels. You're definitely going to need to put on one of the smocks as it can get dirty. I'll be around each of you to start you off, although I think Maggie, you're well practiced by now?"

Maggie smiled proudly. "I am."

Charlotte was the last David came to help, and she concentrated hard to try and get something resembling a pot.

Maggie produced a well formed pot quickly, and was congratulated by David which made her beam. She started another shortly after and then added some embellishments.

At the end when Charlotte was washing her hands and the other students were clearing away their work, David came over to Charlotte. "Are you going home straight away or can I persuade you to stay a little while." He said in a quiet tone.

Charlotte was about to answer when they were interrupted by Maggie holding up her second pot. "Will you fire this tomorrow David?"

David turned around to Maggie with a smile, "Absolutely. We can glaze them next week."

Maggie nodded and just stood there. Charlotte finished washing her hands and gave David a smile and walked away.

Ten minutes later and Dennis and Paul left, leaving Maggie who was tidying up the brushes and glazes.

"No need to do that Maggie." David called over to her.

Maggie turned around. "No problem, just like to make myself useful."

"Very thoughtful of you. See you in the week no doubt."

Maggie finished putting some brushes in a draw then turned around. "I'll be going then. See you." She walked out the door, and David turned to Charlotte. "I thought she'd never leave."

Charlotte laughed. "She does seem to like it here."

"Well, you know, it's my charm and magnetism." David said with humour.

He came over to where Charlotte was stood. Then said in a serious tone. "So are you able to stay a while?"

Charlotte nodded.

Chapter Twenty-One

The next day, at Darren's house, Charlotte and Angus sat opposite Kelly, Darren's partner. She was casually dressed in black tracksuit bottoms and a plain white T-shirt, her hair in a ponytail. Her eyes were red from weeping, with dark shadows beneath.

Next to Kelly was her mother, Laura, a woman of about fifty in jeans and a baggy shirt, who must have had Kelly young. They all had mugs of tea and the silence was oppressive.

Angus wondered how soon he should ask questions. Too soon would seem heartless, too late would prolong the pain.

Charlotte broke the silence first. "We're so sorry for your loss."

Kelly took a tissue from her pocket and dabbed her eyes. "Thanks. I can't believe it. I keep expecting him to walk through the door at any moment."

"Do you remember that we visited the night before last?" Angus asked.

Kelly nodded.

Angus took out his notebook and pen. "We're really grateful to you for talking to us."

"The police said it was about another murder that might be connected?"

Angus nodded. "Yes, the murder of Brian Letterman. We've been hired by Liam Beckett to look into the case. He is trying to clear his name."

Laura sniffed. "But they convicted him in court. I read all about it. People couldn't stop talking about it for weeks."

Angus pressed on. "Do you have any idea who might have killed Darren?"

Kelly shook her head. "No. I want to kill *them*. We were going to get married; we'd been talking about it lately. He hadn't proposed, but he was going to, I'm sure of it." She dabbed her eyes again.

Angus nodded. "Darren called me. He was scared about something, and it was to do with Brian's murder. Do you know why? Did he mention anything to you?"

"No."

"Do you know where he was that night he called me? It was Tuesday at 9pm."

"Tuesday? He was down the pub: the Hare and Hounds. He came back half sozzled. He didn't do that often."

Angus and Charlotte glanced at each other. "Was he there with friends?"

"Well, I suppose you could call them friends. They all meet up, have a drink or five, then roll home. I mean, I don't mind him going out, never did, but it was a Tuesday. He had work the next day and he had to drive, too."

"He didn't mention any names?"

Kelly shook her head. "It was blokes together, you know? I've never been one of those women who question what her man's been up to. I've got a friend like that: she's always on at her partner about who he's been with. It's no way to have a relationship. Everyone needs a bit of space, don't they?"

"Did he say anything to you in the morning about the night before?"

Kelly shook her head.

"And was he stressed about anything lately?"

Laura glanced at Angus, her face troubled.

Angus raised his eyebrows. "Laura?"

She took a deep breath and gave her daughter a sidelong glance.

"Mum?"

"I saw him in Okehampton town centre last week," Laura said. "He was arguing with one of his pub friends. They were in each other's faces, pointing and shouting. Making a right scene, they were. I was driving through town so I couldn't hear what they were arguing about, and by the time I'd parked up and walked there, they'd gone."

"How do you know it was someone from the pub?" Charlotte asked.

"I asked Darren about it when I popped round the day after. He said it was just a mate from the pub, Gary. He said it was nothing to worry about, just a misunderstanding, but I think he was just saying that to stop me asking.

"Can you remember the exact date?"

"It was the fourteenth. I had a hair appointment in town, that's why I was there."

"And it was definitely Gary Reid?"

"Yeah, it was him. I only know him by sight, we've never spoken."

Angus looked at the questions he'd written in his note-book earlier. "Could you tell me what happened up to

Darren leaving the house on the morning that he was killed?"

Kelly dabbed her eyes again. "The alarm went off at 5.30am as usual, and he was out the house by 6am. He loved his job and thought the world of Lord Farnley. That was the last time I saw him." She hiccupped.

"Did he have a computer?" Charlotte asked.

"Yeah, the police took his laptop. They think there might be evidence on it. Dunno what, though, he hardly used it."

Charlotte's face fell, her mouth formed a tight, unhappy line.

Kelly continued. "Look, I don't know about Brian's murder, and Darren never really spoke about it. He didn't start working for Lord Farnley until after Brian was murdered. He didn't even know Brian. Why would he know anything about his murder?"

They left and Charlotte waited until they were at Angus's car before speaking. "We need to talk to Gary again, but he won't want to talk to us. Why don't you let me go on my own? He might be more receptive to a woman."

Angus shook his head. "I'm not putting you at risk. He was rude and aggressive last time we saw him."

"I'll bring Grigore. He'll protect me. He can stay out of sight, and step in if needed."

"Gary won't tell you anything."

"We have to try, though. Maybe he has a girlfriend or a wife we can talk to."

"Even if he has, it doesn't mean they'll know anything. We'll have to think of another way to talk to him."

Charlotte's face brightened. "I know! We can ply him with booze in the pub."

Angus considered her suggestion. "Actually, that's not a

bad idea. We could go to the pub when we know he's there, then buy him drinks and food."

"Great," said Charlotte. "We can stake out his place tonight and follow him to the pub." Then she remembered that she'd promised to see David. "Um, actually, I can't tonight. I'm meeting a friend."

"We can try tomorrow," said Angus. "I wouldn't mind a night off, anyway. After yesterday, I need to run, and it's the club's 5K Quayside run tonight."

Chapter Twenty-Two

When Charlotte got home, she found Helena, her Romanian best friend and housekeeper unloading the dishwasher. "How was day?" Helena asked.

"Confusing," said Charlotte.

They kissed each other on the cheek, then Charlotte opened the fridge, took out a bottle of green smoothie and drank from it.

Helena went to the cupboard, got a glass, and handed it to her a look of annoyance on her face.

"Thanks. The case we're working on is a real puzzle. Did you hear about the murder on the news, the one near Okehampton? That's related to what we're looking into."

"Yez, terrible. And Mr Angus! Poor man being questioned by police like he some kind of criminal. He last man who kill anyone. You should go around round to his house later to cheer him up. Take food. Vay to man's heart is through stomach."

Charlotte grimaced. "Surely that's just an old wives' tale?"

"Wives' tales usually true, zo." Helena put away the last plate and closed the dishwasher door. "You no busy tonight, go to Mr Angus. You never know, tonight maybe the night." She winked.

"I had plans, actually, but Angus comes first." Charlotte thought about David. She'd seen him last night and had stayed a few hours after the class. Seeing him was starting to become a habit. Was it all too much? He was such a nice man, and despite that, all she could think about was how much she'd rather be with Angus.

Maybe she could see both of them. Drop in on David, then head over to Angus. Yes, that would work. She messaged Angus to see if he wanted company after his run.

He replied quickly:

Just about to start my run, then going to pub with the other runners.

Well that was a warning to stay away if ever she heard one. Hopefully David would be more enthusiastic. She started to compose a text, but Helena eyed her suspiciously.

"What you up to lately?" said Helena. "Grigore tell me he drop you off at pottery place other night and it not lesson night."

Charlotte's jaw dropped, and she wondered what to tell Helena. Helena never approved of her flings, although it had been a while since she'd had one. "You have to promise not to tell me off," she began.

Helena put her hand on her hip. "What you do? Create special pottery?"

That was one way of putting it. "Er, no, not quite. Me and the man who teaches pottery have been getting to know each other better."

Helena blinked as she took this in. "I thought you love Angus?"

"I do, but he's not interested."

Helena stared at Charlotte. "Who is he? I check he good man!"

"David's a pottery expert. He's *really* good with his hands. We've only just started seeing each other, and I don't know if it's even a thing. I just wanted the company of a man for a bit... I have needs."

"Maybe Mr Angus vill be jealous if he find out you vith other man. You tell him?"

"God, no!" She considered Helena's words. "But maybe it would make him jealous. That would be a good thing, right?"

"Tell him how you feel. Honesty best zing."

Charlotte sighed. "Easy for you to say, Helena. We've been over this countless times."

"Ve have, yes. And still you say nothing."

Charlotte went into the office and sat at her desk. Helena had put her post on the keyboard: a letter from the water company trying to sell insurance for plumbing and a letter without her name and address on the front. She opened it and pulled out a single piece of paper with a single sentence written in pen.

Stay away. You've been warned.

· · ·

"What the..." Charlotte turned the sheet over; there was nothing on the other side. *It's just like the one Angus received.* She took a photo of it and WhatsApped it to him. *I got one too,* she typed.

She expected Angus to text back, but he phoned straight away. He sounded out of breath. "When did it arrive?"

"I've no idea, but it wasn't sent through the mail. It had my name and address on the front, but no stamp - just like yours."

"Mine was hand-delivered too, with no name on it."

"Is there a way we can get them checked for finger-prints?" Charlotte asked.

"There are companies who have labs that can do it privately. I've used one last year. We can send them both off tomorrow. Make sure no-one else touches the letter."

"I will." She put the letter down as though it was on fire.

"Make sure Grigore stays with you tonight and that your CCTV is on."

"You think they might do something to harm me?" The stress in Charlotte's voice was palpable.

There was silence for a moment. "No, no this is just scare tactics again. But it never hurts to be cautious."

"Okay."

"Alright see you in the morning." Angus ended the call, and Charlotte looked at her phone. She wanted him to say they should meet up and he'd stay over. She didn't even get a chance to tell him she was scared. Because she was. It was just like a few months ago when she was in danger then.

She sighed. Everything was getting super stressful again. Her first thought was to go over to Angus's house anyway and wait until he got home but that could be hours.

She messaged David and he responded quickly.

. . .

Just finished an evening class. Come over if you like. Or I can come over to you?

The lure of another night of passion and getting away from any danger was alluring, but she didn't want him in her house just yet. He'd want to know how she could afford such a big house, and then he'd know she was rich. She wanted him to get to know her without the multi-million-aire label.

She messaged back: *I'll come to you. See you soon. X*

Grigore to drove her over, dropped her around the corner again and she arrived with a bottle of wine. David showed her in, and greeted her with a kiss on the cheek, which turned into a full on kiss and a repeat of the other night.

Chapter Twenty-Three

Next morning, Angus arrived and they sat at their usual places in the study, with their coffees.

"Penny for them?" said Angus, and she jumped.

"Sorry, I was miles away. I was thinking about last night." She felt her face warming.

"You shouldn't worry about the letter, you know. They're just trying to spook us. But I do want you to strengthen your security. Can you get Grigore to stay here for a while?"

Charlotte raised her eyebrows. "So you want *me* to get extra security, but *you* won't."

Angus sipped his coffee and said nothing.

"Anyway, how are you after your arrest? That must have fazed you a bit."

Angus's face darkened. "I wasn't officially arrested, but I'm fine." He stood up and walked to the conspiracy board. "I'm not sure why you're asking me this, it's been two days."

"You're not fine. I can tell. I'm concerned about you."

He studied the board, shoulders set.

Charlotte went over and touched his arm. A week ago, she'd have gone round to his house with a takeaway and a bottle of wine to cheer him up. Now, she was seeing David for sex most nights. She felt a pang of guilt and she couldn't understand why. He'd been the one who'd turned her down last night. She had nothing to feel guilty about.

Angus took a sip of coffee and sighed. "I'd be lying if I said I wasn't bothered about it. When I got home, the reality of being the chief suspect of a murder hit me. It was extremely annoying."

"Don't worry, Hugo will sort everything out. He never loses."

Angus adjusted his tie. "About Hugo..."

Charlotte held her hands up in mock surrender. "I know you're going to go on about the money, but if it makes you feel better, remember that it's not about you. It's about me and my recovery. I need you out of jail and investigating with me. I'd go nuts if I didn't have this work."

Angus looked her in the eye. "I knew you were going to say that. You do know that I can never repay you?"

Charlotte made a dismissive motion with her hand. "This has never been about money. I need the work, Angus. How many times do I have to tell you?"

"A few more," Angus said with a half-smile. "I'm annoyed at myself for letting it happen."

Charlotte stared at him. "What? It wasn't your fault!"

"I know, but I can't help blaming myself."

"This has really rattled you, hasn't it?"

Angus paused, weighing his words. "I feel like I did when I decided to quit the force. Really, really angry."

Charlotte wanted to put her arms around him and comfort him. But the memory of him rejecting her kiss on the day they first met stopped her. "You know, you should take a leaf out of my book and get back to work. It does wonders."

"All right."

"Give me your letter and I'll send both off for forensic analysis. Then we should talk to the landlord of the pub again. Darren was in his pub two nights before he was murdered; maybe he heard something. And we need to speak to Gary, of course."

"We could go tonight."

"That means we've got all day with nothing to do. I think we should track down Gary and try to catch him unawares."

"That could take ages. He might not go anywhere."

Charlotte glanced at her computer. "Or he might go to the farm-supply shop today."

Angus's shoulders tensed. "You hacked his computer?"

"Why would you even think that? I promised you I wouldn't, and I haven't."

"How do you know, then?"

"Facebook. Most of his profile and his posts are public. Classic social media mistake! Total numpty. He's meeting a friend there at 1pm. There's a book launch for a friend who's got a book out: a humorous memoir of farming, apparently. See, I found it out without hacking him." She looked triumphant.

It was Angus's turn to hold up his hands. "All right. Let's go to the farm-supply shop and see what we can learn about his argument with Darren."

Chapter Twenty-Four

The farm-supply shop was an ugly metal building with a large shop logo and one small window, sitting on a small industrial estate just outside Okehampton.

Inside, it was similar to a DIY store, except that the products were all farm-related: fence posts, chicken wire, bags of fertiliser, a myriad of gadgets and outdoor clothing.

Near the main door was a long table with a display banner which read: *The Ploughman's Lunch: A Comedic Memoir of Life on the Farm,* by Allan Watson. Underneath the title was a larger-than-life photo of the author holding a copy of the book. Behind the table, on which was a few stacks of books, stood Allan Watson, alone.

"From the Facebook posts, I thought lots of people would be here," Charlotte whispered. She looked at her watch. "We're early. But only by about ten minutes."

"We can talk to the author," said Angus. "As there's no one at the table, he'll be more likely to open up."

They headed over to the table and Allan Watson smiled at them. He was at least sixty, well over six feet tall with wire-framed glasses he was dressed in a pale grey suit, but no tie which gave him a smart-casual look. "Hello, are you here for the book signing?"

Charlotte picked up a copy of the book. The cover showed a cartoon bull chasing a cartoon farmer who looked like Allan. She handed it to him with her cash payment. "Yes, we are. Would you sign this to me, please? I'm Charlotte."

"Of course." Allan took the book from her, delved into his inside jacket pocket and took out a fountain pen. He bent over the table and signed the title page.

Charlotte took the book when he'd finished. "Thank you. So what gave you the inspiration for writing the book?"

"Oh you know, I've always wanted to write a book. It's wonderful seeing my name in print, you know?" Allan looked rather bewildered.

"And what made you decide on a memoir?"

"It was a conversation at the pub actually. Me and a few friends were exchanging drunken anecdotes and my friend Gary suggested putting them all in a book."

Charlotte's interest was piqued. "Gary Reid?"

Allan smiled. "Why, yes! Do you know him?"

"A little."

Allan clapped his hands together. "Fabulous, a mutual friend! He should be here any minute."

Angus had wandered to the other end of the table and was leafing through a copy of the book.

"What a coincidence," said Charlotte. "We can catch up. Do you often meet him in the pub?"

"A couple of times a month. Not as often as I'd like, really. Elderly mother, you see, she needs a lot of TLC. I get the occasional night off, though." Allan looked past Charlotte to the shop entrance. "Speak of the devil – here's the man himself."

Charlotte glanced round, then looked at Angus. "I'll come and chat to him in a bit. That'll give you time to sign his copy..." She made a beeline for Angus and they moved to the clothing section to watch surreptitiously.

Allan and Gary chatted for a few minutes, then Allan signed a book for Gary, who wandered off.

"Now's our chance." Angus followed Gary to the back of the store, with Charlotte close behind.

They found him browsing the sheep castration pliers. "Gary, we need to talk," said Angus.

It took Gary a few moments to realise who they were. Then he scowled. "What do you want? I told you I didn't want to talk to you."

Charlotte stepped forward and spoke softly. "We just want to ask you a few things about Darren. You were seen arguing with him the week before he was murdered."

"What? Who by?"

"A witness. There's no point in denying it. It was in the middle of Okehampton High Street."

Gary lifted his chin. "I had a row with him, yeah, but he was the one who confronted me. He accused me of poaching, the stupid bastard."

"I take it you didn't like that?" Angus asked.

"Course I didn't. 'Cos I didn't do it."

"What exactly did he accuse you of?" Angus asked.

"Setting traps for hares."

"Why did he think it was you?"

"Dunno, but it wasn't. Hares are protected. I ain't interested in trapping them or any other animal."

"He must have had some reason to accuse you, though." Angus commented.

Gary shrugged. "Probably heard it from someone down the pub who doesn't like me."

"So you argued in the street. Then what?"

"I grabbed him by the shirt, but that's all. I didn't hit him, though I was tempted. He didn't have a shred of proof it was me, and he knew it."

Angus looked at Charlotte and she shrugged. "Where were you on the morning Darren was killed?" he asked.

Gary's eyes narrowed. "You're trying to pin Darren's murder on me, aren't you."

Angus shook his head. "We're asking questions so that we can eliminate you as a suspect."

That seemed to placate Gary. "I was at home and I can prove it." He paused for a moment. "My girlfriend stayed over that night."

Angus raised his eyebrows. "She doesn't live with you permanently?"

"No. She's got a teenage son with learning difficulties. She stays with me when he's with his father."

"What's her name?"

"I ain't telling you that. You're not the police and it's none of your business." He stepped back. "Is that all? 'Cos I got things to do."

Angus nodded. "It is. Thank you for talking to us."

Gary grunted, picked up a sheep castrator and stalked off.

"Do you believe him?" Charlotte asked, as they watched him disappear down an aisle which said *Animal Feed*.

"For now. Unless something else comes up, we have to. But can you check his social media accounts and see if he does have a girlfriend?"

Charlotte smiled. "Consider it done."

Chapter Twenty-Five

Charlotte looked up from her tablet computer. She was sitting in Angus's lounge, cross-legged on the sofa. "I've looked through Gary's social media posts again and there are some photos of him with a woman. They seem to meet up most Sundays for a lunch date. He's tagged her in the posts, and he's smiling at her in the photos. They eat well, judging by the photos of their food they post."

"He probably wasn't lying, then. But we should contact her and ask, just to confirm his alibi. I don't think he did it, though. I have a hunch."

Charlotte pointed to the screen. "I asked Mark to get me access to Darren's laptop. He couldn't give me direct access, but he sent the report. I thought this was interesting..."

Angus sat next to her on the sofa. "What am I looking for?"

Charlotte pointed to the middle of the screen. "This is a list of the websites he visited. Some are of no interest, but this one....

Angus read the text aloud. "Devon County Council Planning Department."

"I'm not sure what significance it has yet. But he visited it every day for a month."

Angus frowned. "And you think this is significant because...?"

"Because Brian visited the same website in the days leading up to his murder."

Angus considered this. "OK, so they both visited the Devon County Council planning website before they died. It might be a coincidence."

"Who visits the council's planning website, though? Do you?"

Angus shrugged. "Never been on it. Even when I put in planning permission for my flats, I had the architect do all that."

"Me neither. And I bet if we ask everyone we know, there'll be hardly anyone who has visited it. Yet both murder victims had been on there recently."

"All right," said Angus. "Let's work on the assumption that they were both looking into a planning issue. What might that be? A neighbour with an illegal extension or building? Maybe they'd heard a neighbour was putting in planning permission, but they hadn't done it yet."

"Or it could be something commercial," said Charlotte.

"We need to ask their closest relatives if they talked about it," Angus said decisively. "We should pay Jessica another visit. Brian might have mentioned something to her about the planning website."

Charlotte looked sceptical. "I doubt you'll get much out of her."

"She might help, though, and we can ask her if she still has Brian's laptop, too. I still want you to look through it."

Charlotte sighed. "All right."

That evening, they went to Jessica's house. As soon as she opened the door and saw them her face darkened. "What the... Piss off. I told you before. I'm not going to help you."

Charlotte spoke first. "Please, Jessica, we really need to speak to you. It won't take a moment."

She stabbed a finger at them. "I told you to stay away, didn't I? What part of piss off don't you understand? If you don't go away, I'm calling the police and reporting you for harassment."

"We're not trying to harass you," said Angus, patiently. "We just want to ask you whether your father mentioned anything about looking into planning permission before he died."Jessica stared at him. "Planning permission? Why would he be looking into that?"

"We don't know. We wondered whether he'd mentioned it."

"No," she said immediately. "Look, you're not tricking me into anything. I'm not helping you get Liam Beckett off the hook."

"It isn't like that: we're just trying to get to the truth. So he never mentioned anything about planning permission?"

"I said no, didn't I?"

"You're sure?"

She put her hands on her hips. "Yeah."

"One more thing... Do you still have your father's laptop?"

Her eyes narrowed. "Why?"

"Because if you do, we'd like to look at it."

She laughed. "You're kidding, right?"

"No."

"I'm not letting you have his laptop!"

"You still have it, then?"

"What?" She scowled at Angus. "Stop trying to catch me out. Yeah, I've got it. So what?"

"Have you used it at all?"

"No. It was Dad's. Besides, it's really old and slow."

"Can we borrow it?" Angus asked.

"No."

"We promise we'll return it. We just want to look at it." Charlotte said.

She snorted. "So you can find something to get Liam out of prison?"

"Or we might find something that proves he did it."

Jessica stood silent, thinking that over. "I'm not letting you have it," she said, stepping back.

Charlotte sighed. "All right. How much do you want for it?"

Angus gave her a disapproving look.

"What?" said Jessica.

"I said how much do you want for it?"

"I'm not selling it." Jessica folded her arms.

Charlotte raised her eyebrows. "Really? Everyone has their price."

"I don't."

Charlotte narrowed her eyes. "I think you do." She paused. "How about a thousand pounds?"

Jessica's mouth fell open, then she drew herself up and pursed her lips. "Five thousand."

Charlotte was caught between admiration and smugness that Jessica had named her price. The truth was that Charlotte would have paid her ten times that amount. She wasn't going to let Jessica know that, though.

"Done. Fetch the laptop, and I'll transfer the money into your bank account."

Jessica stayed put. "You'd better not be scamming me."

"I'm not scamming you. Go and get the laptop, show me it was your father's, I'll transfer the money and we'll take the laptop with us. You'd better get your bank account details, too."

Jessica weighed this up, then opened the door and motioned them inside.

Jessica took them into the lounge, where they sat on the settee. A compact yet well-organised room, there was a comfortable three-seater sofa opposite a modest flat-screen TV on a wooden stand. Next to the window a small coffee table surrounded by a couple of cushioned chairs. The walls were painted a light cream, with a few framed photos.

She disappeared upstairs, returning a few minutes later with a clunky old laptop and a bank statement. "This is it," she said. "I don't have a charger for it, and I haven't used it since the police gave it back."

"Do you have his mobile phone too?" Charlotte asked.

"Maybe."

"How much do you want for that?"

"Another 5K."

"Two."

"Three."

"Done. Go and get it."

Jessica handed her the bank statement. "That's my bank account number," she said, pointing.

"I'll get the transfer ready."

Jessica left the room, taking the laptop with her.

Charlotte took out her mobile phone and opened her banking app.

Angus's voice cut through the silence. "Are we going to have another argument about you paying everyone off?"

Charlotte looked up from her phone. "I don't know. Are we?"

Angus opened his mouth to speak, then closed it. Charlotte returned her attention to her phone.

Jessica returned soon afterwards with the laptop and a smartphone. Charlotte made the bank transfer and Jessica checked her balance on her phone. "Thank you," she said.

Charlotte took hold of the items. "No, thank you."

Jessica huffed. "Well, I need the money, don't I? Dad didn't leave me anything, not after I'd paid for his funeral."

"Was your father ever in debt?"

Jessica shook her head. "No. He was on good enough money, but the cost of living these days took its toll on him. Living on your own is expensive."

"Yes," said Charlotte. "Look, thank you for these."

"If you find any photos of Dad, will you give me a copy?"

"Of course," said Charlotte.

Once Jessica had seen them out, Angus walked silently to the car. Buying people off seemed to be Charlotte's new habit, now that she couldn't hack everyone and anything. He wasn't sure which was worse. He also wondered how he would ever complete another case without her knowledge and her financial backing. In the police, he had had access to all sorts of resources: databases with people's backgrounds, government information, criminal records, previous addresses. And he'd had the right to take people's property, like computers, if it might contain evidence. He'd relied on those things back then. Now, though, he had none of that, and he had to rely on using persuasion or finding some kind of workaround.

Except when Charlotte hacked into things or threw money at problems.

In the car, he found his voice. "Look, Charlotte, when I said I'd like you to look at the laptop I didn't expect you to pay thousands of pounds for it."

Charlotte shrugged. "I know. But like I keep saying, that amount of money is small potatoes. And no, I won't run out."

Angus sat in silence for a moment, then started the car. He still didn't like it, but there wasn't much else he could do.

Back at Charlotte's, she quickly found a charger that matched the laptop and set to work. The laptop sprang to life, and she plugged it into her own computer to download the contents.

Angus stood gazing at the conspiracy board, wondering what they would do if Charlotte found nothing.

"This is a very old, very cheap laptop." Charlotte commented as she typed. "And very slow." She drummed her fingers on the table waiting for the operating system to start.

Angus continued to scrutinise the board. "Do you think you'll find anything that the police didn't?"

"Depends how thorough the police were. If they assumed that Liam did it, they wouldn't have bothered to investigate the laptop in depth. But if there is anything on here, I'll find it."

"I don't doubt it."

She started her pre-written search program do most of the work. Then sat back and waited.

Sometime later, Charlotte looked up from the computer. "I can't find anything significant on here."

Angus looked up from the court report he was rereading."You're sure?"

"Absolutely. The police report is completely accurate. I ran all the files on the computer through a scanner to check for hidden or secret data, but it found nothing. His internet search history was almost nonexistent, but as the police evidence showed, he visited the council planning department website a number of times in the days leading up to his murder."

"What about the phone?"

She smiled. "I was just coming to that...The phone is more interesting. He used Messenger a lot when he was at work, all work related and nothing unusual. Just things like how many wooden posts they need for a fence. Nothing very notable. However, in his photos are a number of pictures of an area of land. A couple fields. According to the photos' metadata, it's situated to the north of a small village called Chulmton."

Angus smiled. "That sounds like something out of a children's TV show I watched when I was small."

"Mmm. And something else you might like to know if that the area of land is owned by Lord Farnley." Charlotte smiled as Angus's eyes widened. "Anyway, one of the very last websites he visited, along with the planning website, belongs to a company called Beamont Holdings. He also took a screenshot of their website on his phone on the same day as he took the photos of that piece of land."

Angus mused. "Beamont Holdings sounds generic. What do they do?"

"They have fingers in lots of pies. Mainly housing developments, with some startups."

"I take it you've done a search on them?"

"Yep, a full company search. Finding out who owns

Beamont Holdings isn't a easy. It's actually owned by another company, which in turn is owned by another company. Eventually, though, I've dug out the names of three men, all speculators. They're millionaires who have been involved in countless developments over the years. They mainly deal with office buildings now, but they started off by buying up former mills in the north of England and turning them into flats. Then they moved onto more commercial sites: retail parks, office complexes, stuff like that."

"It can't be a coincidence that Brian was looking at the planning website and had a screenshot of this company's website. Not on the same day."

"I don't think so, either."

"Can you search the planning website for that company?"

Charlotte nodded and began typing. A few minutes later, she looked up. "No sign of them."

"What about the other companies they're associated with?" Angus asked. "The ones which own them?"

"I tried those too, it looked promising but it's a dead end. There was nothing."

Angus put his finger on his lips and pondered. A moment later, his phone rang. He frowned at it and answered.

"Mr Darrow? This is Martin Hill, Liam Beckett's solicitor."

Angus moved to the other side of the room. "How can I help?"

"Mr Beckett would like you to visit him in prison as soon as possible. Normally you'd have to book in, but as he's adamant that he wants to see you sooner, I can take you in. Could you come tomorrow?"

"Er, sure." Angus's brow furrowed as he wondered what Liam wanted to speak to him about so urgently.

"Good. I'll meet you at the prison at 9am."

The call ended and Angus relayed the conversation to Charlotte.

"Didn't the lawyer say why Liam wants to see you?" asked Charlotte, looking puzzled. "And does he want me to come too?"

"The lawyer didn't mention you, but you could come along," said Angus. "If Liam doesn't want you there, you could always wait outside."

Chapter Twenty-Six

The next morning, Charlotte and Angus stood in the waiting area outside the prison visitors' room with Martin Hill. He was a tall, serious man in a grey suit that, despite his height, was a little too long for him.

The men shook hands and Angus introduced Charlotte, again using only her first name. Mr Hill gave Charlotte a disapproving look over his glasses and said nothing.

When they were allowed into the visiting room, Liam Beckett was already sitting at one of the tables. He looked up as soon as they entered and got slowly to his feet. "Mr Hill, thanks for sorting this," he said in a grateful tone. The shadows under his eyes suggested at least one night of poor sleep.

Mr Hill sat down and Charlotte and Angus followed suit. Liam sat down too, and stared at Charlotte, his face angry.

Angus pushed his glasses up his nose. "What did you want to talk to us about?"

Liam met Angus's eyes, then pointed his finger at Charlotte. "Her." There was a long pause. "She's that bastard policeman's sister, and you didn't tell me."

Angus had known that at some point Liam would probably find out about Charlotte. He'd thought through the arguments in his head, ready for it. He didn't like hiding things. "She is," he said.

"Why didn't you tell me? Do you think I would have spent my money on you if I'd known? You've well and truly shafted me."

Charlotte opened her mouth to speak but Angus put his hand on her arm. "I knew that you would have an issue with Charlotte helping with the case, because of her brother. I didn't tell you because Charlotte works for me. I take the lead on all cases."

Charlotte nodded. "He does. He doesn't like it when I use my initiative."

Angus gave her a sidelong glance. Her face was completely neutral.

Liam leaned forward and pointed at Angus. "I've been paying you my life savings, and all along, the sister of the plod who put me away has been 'helping' you!" He put air quotes around the word 'helping'.

"I have been helping him," said Charlotte. "And while Mark Lockwood is my brother, I won't let that cloud my judgement. If he put you away and you're innocent, I'm more than happy to expose that. He's a good man, despite what you may think. In fact, he knows that I've been helping Angus, and he's done nothing to stop either of us getting to the truth."

Liam looked incredulous. "*He's* been helping you?"

"He's busy enough with other cases," said Angus. "However, if he wanted to make it difficult for us, he could. And he hasn't."

Liam's shoulders relaxed. He looked at Mr Hill, who looked at the sheet of paper in front of him. "Mr Beckett asked me to do background checks on you both, and it seems Miss Lockwood here is a multimillionaire. Is that correct?" He raised his eyebrows at her, his expression still disapproving.

Charlotte blinked twice, slowly. "That is correct."

"Why are you working as a private investigator, then?" asked Liam, frowning. "Do you get some sort of kick out of seeing desperate people?"

Charlotte shook her head. "Not at all. You see, not long after acquiring my fortune I discovered that my husband was cheating on me, and my world collapsed. Working with Angus has given me a new purpose and has transformed my mental health. That's why I work with him. Plus I'm a cybersecurity expert, which helps."

Liam put his hand over his eyes.

Charlotte leaned forward. "Liam, we're getting close. We know you didn't kill Brian. Please give us some more time."

Liam looked at Angus. "Is that true?"

Angus nodded. "I'm sure you aren't guilty. We've had poison-pen letters warning us off, which shows that we're on the right track. The more we dig, the more we find. And we're sure that Darren's murder is related." Angus held Liam's gaze. "I understand your reservations about Charlotte, but you don't need to worry. She's on your side, just as much as I am."

Liam let out a long breath. "All right. It's just so hard, sat here in prison unable to do anything. I'm betting my life's savings on you two. If you don't succeed, I don't know how much longer I can go on. I regret being so at odds with

Brian now. I'm sitting here, day in, day out, going over all the petty arguments we had. It seems ridiculous now."

Charlotte leaned back in her chair. "Is there anything you want to ask me before we go? I mean, to reassure you that my brother being the 'plod' who put you here has no influence on our search for the real killer?"

Liam shook his head and laughed, without humour. "No."

Chapter Twenty-Seven

In the prison car park, Angus turned to Charlotte. "That went better than I thought."

Charlotte grinned. "It must be my good looks and charm."

Angus smiled back. "I actually think it was. Let me make you lunch, and we'll discuss what to do next."

Charlotte nodded and they got in the car.

Angus drove them to his house. As he let them in, he frowned at a letter on the doormat. He retrieved it and held it up.

"A plain white envelope with nothing written on it. Remind you of anything?" He opened the envelope and pulled out a single sheet. "Yep, it's another one."

He read out the letter. *"This is your final warning. Stop now, unless you want to end up like Darren."*

"That's terrible," said Charlotte. "We definitely need to report this to the police. I'll take a photo and send it to Mark. Do you think they've sent me one too?"

Angus walked into the kitchen and Charlotte followed. "Probably. If they have, you should step up your security."

"So should you. They're threatening to kill you."

"This isn't the first time."

Charlotte's eyes widened. "Really?"

Angus filled the kettle with water and switched it on. "Gang members threatened me when I was in the police. I sent Grace and Rhona to her parents for a few weeks until it had blown over." He leaned against the worktop.

"Well, I'll get extra security and then you can come and stay at mine again."

Angus looked up and shook his head. "I don't think that's a good idea."

"Why not?"

"I won't allow myself to be intimidated by them."

"But I need protection?"

"You're only in this situation because you work for me. So yes, you need protection. Promise me you'll get some."

Charlotte frowned. "I'll get Grigore to stay for a few days. He won't mind: his girlfriend is away at the moment."

"That's a good start. But think about further protection."

The kettle boiled, and Angus made them tea. Charlotte sent a photo of the letter to Mark on WhatsApp. "What next, then?" she said, sipping her drink.

"We need to speak to Lord Farnley about Darren. He's his employer: maybe he saw or heard something. I want to know about the land Brian took photos of."

"OK. He wasn't very helpful last time, and he didn't have any information. But it is suspicious that two men who were murdered both worked for him."

"Generally, coincidences aren't actually coincidences," said Angus.

Charlotte raised her eyebrows. "You think he did it?"

"I'm not saying that. I'm saying that it's something to look into."

Charlotte nodded. "And they were both gamekeepers. If only we could find out what Darren meant to tell you when he called."

"If he didn't write it down, we'll never know."

"That's an interesting thought." Charlotte put her cup down and took out her phone. "I'll see if there's anything on the internet."

Angus frowned. "He won't have posted anything on social media. He wouldn't even speak to us."

"That's true, but I'll check anyway. There could be some info about who he hung out with that night. And we need to speak to William, the landlord of the pub again, to find out more about the night before Darren died.Which shall we do first?"

"The pub."

Chapter Twenty-Eight

Angus drove them to the Hare and Hounds. It was busier than the last time they'd visited, which was surprising as it was only two in the afternoon, when most people would be at work. The weather was still hot, so most people were outside in the beer garden, or sitting at the picnic-style tables outside the entrance.

Inside, it took a moment for their eyes to adjust to the darkness, but once they were standing at the bar, a woman appeared. "What can I get you?" She was in her fifties, with grey hair tied back in a slick ponytail, wearing smart black trousers and a white shirt.

"Is William around?" Angus asked.

"Sorry love, he's out at the moment. Can I help?" She glanced at Charlotte, then back to Angus.

"Were you working here the night before Darren Gilford was murdered? I believe he came in for a few drinks?"

"Yeah, I was working." She put a hand on one of the beer pump handles.

"Did you see Darren that night?"

She blinked twice at him, something Angus had seen a few times from Charlotte. There was a long pause before she answered. "Yeah, I did. Terrible what happened to him. Who are you?"

"We're private investigators."

"Oh yeah? That must be interesting work." The woman fluttered her eyelashes at Angus and Charlotte felt jealously sear through her. She suppressed the urge to put her arm around Angus as a signal to the woman to back off.

Angus cleared his throat. "Did you see him?"

"Yeah, he was here and drinking far too much. I had to take his car keys off him. Not that he'd ever driven back drunk before, but I look after the punters, you see." She smiled at Angus and he nodded back. "Would you like a drink?"

"Er, not at the moment. Can you tell me what happened the night Darren was here? Did you see or hear him make any phone calls, for instance?"

She considered his question. "Not that I remember. I mean, everyone's always staring at their phones now, aren't they."

"Who was he drinking with?"

"He was on his own most of the night. I think he chatted to a couple of the other regulars, as well as William." She tilted her head and fluttered her eyelashes at Angus again. "Look, are you going to at least have a drink, with all this questioning?"

"Er, OK. I'll have a Coke."

"Diet or full fat?"

"Diet."

"Gotta keep that toned body trim, eh?" She said, her

eyes on Angus's torso. Then she took a glass from under the counter, picked up the soda tap and filled it.

Charlotte decided that, while she wanted to pour Angus's drink over the woman, Angus would get much further with his questioning if she made herself scarce. "I'll be outside," she muttered, and left the pub.

Chapter Twenty-Nine

The barmaid set Angus's drink down on the bar towel. "I'm Jo, by the way."

Angus took out his wallet.

"No, no. On me." She leaned forward, resting her elbows on the bar. "So, what else do you want to know?"

"Do you know what Darren and William were talking about?"

Jo shrugged. "Dunno, but they were talking for a short time. I remember getting annoyed at William, sat on his backside talking and leaving all the work to me. Don't get me wrong, I'm not work-shy, but this is a big pub. It needs more than one of us behind the bar, you know?"

"And William didn't mention what they talked about?"

"Nope. He never tells me anything. We're not friends – I'm only working here until I can find something better."

She smiled at Angus, then added, "Oh, William went outside for a bit, because he's a smoker. That was when Darren was on his phone. Then William came back when he was talking and Darren ended the call."

"You saw all that?"

"Yeah, there was a lull at that point. Darren was agitated. He was like that all evening, but worse after he'd spoken to William."

"And you don't know why?"

Jo narrowed her eyes. "You trying to pin Darren's murder on William?" Then she laughed.

Angus picked up his drink and took a sip. "Not at all, just trying to get to the facts. Can you remember what time it was when you saw Darren making that call?"

"Around 9pm."

"And is there anything else you can tell me about that night? Anything that stuck out, that seemed unusual?"

Jo pursed her lips. "Not that I can think of."

Angus downed the rest of the drink. "Thanks for that."

"No problem. Give me your card, will you, in case I think of anything later."

Angus took his wallet out and handed her a card.

Jo scanned it. "Angus Darrow. Nothing else, except your phone number. That's very mysterious." She smiled at him.

"I thought that putting Private Investigator on my card sounded pretentious. Well, thanks again, Jo. You've been very helpful."

"Bye, Angus Darrow." She gave him a little wave as he left.

Outside, Angus looked around for Charlotte. He'd noticed when she left, and wasn't entirely sure why she had gone. He found her sitting at a picnic bench, her eyes closed and her face lifted to the sun.

She opened her eyes as he approached. "Was she any help?"

Angus sat down opposite her. "A bit. She remembered Darren in the pub that night. Apparently he spent some time talking to William, the landlord and he also made a call. She didn't know what they talked about, but from the sound of it, Darren called me from the pub that night. The timing was right, too: about 9pm."

"So you've pinned that down," said Charlotte.

"And he was interrupted by William coming back to sit with him. That's why he ended the call." Angus sighed. "I wish I knew what they'd been talking about. It stands to reason that he didn't want William to overhear him on the phone, but Jo said they were talking for a while."

Charlotte smiled. "Jo?"

"Yes, that's the barmaid's name."

Charlotte chuckled. "She fancies you."

Angus cleared his throat and adjusted his tie.

"So, did *Jo* have any other helpful info?"

"No, she didn't."

"What next, then?"

"Lord Farnley. There's no point hanging around here."

Charlotte nodded and stood up. "Let's hope Lord Farnley is more helpful this time."

Just as they got in the car, Charlotte's phone pinged. She took it out and looked at it. "Well, that's interesting..."

Angus looked across at her. "What is?"

"I wrote a web crawler to search the dark web for all the major players in this case. It's found something. I'll take a look."

They moved to inside Angus's car, then she delved into her bag for her laptop and opened it. Angus leaned over to watch.

She opened a TOR browser, typed in an address then clicked a few times.

"It looks like Brian's VLOG." She looked at the screen,

analysing what she saw. "It seems he posted to it not every-day, but often enough. It's some sort of personal journal."

She clicked on the final video posted and it started play-ing. The video appeared to be his house, from the furniture in the background, it was a living room. He looked tired and drawn.

"I've uncovered something big." Brian sighed and rubbed his face with both hands then faced the camera again.

"My boss, Lord Farnley, is working with a company called Beamont Holdings. They're trying to get planning permission for a massive housing estate on his land." He looked away briefly. "I found out a few days ago, and when I confronted Lord Farnley he denied it at first then offered a cut if I kept it quiet. At first I couldn't believe they'd get planning permission for it, but they've got insiders at the council. Someone who works at the planning department is preparing the way to persuade councillors and civil servants to build a new town there." There was a long pause. "I'm scared—they want to destroy a beautiful part of the farm and I've said I can't go along with it. I don't know what they're going to do. They've been hiding it to make sure the locals don't have enough time to put up too much opposition."

Brian jumped at a loud banging sounded off-screen. A man's voice shouted, "Come out here, you bastard."

It was Liam's voice.

"That's Liam." Brian sighed. "I'll go and sort him out." Brian leaned forward and the video stopped.

A few seconds later, it started again. Brian sat in front of the screen as before. "Sorry. That was my idiot neighbour accusing me of something. As usual. I sent him packing with a fist."

Angus looked at Charlotte. "Pause it for a moment." Charlotte pressed the spacebar and the video stopped. "This was filmed on the night he died."

Charlotte nodded. "The day and time uploaded was the night he died. Look." She pointed to the date stamp next to the video. "This proves that it wasn't Liam. He's been and gone, and now Brian is back recording."

Angus shook his head. "Even if the police saw this, they'd argue that Liam could have come back. They have the blood evidence, remember. And he was stabbed in the middle of the night, after the altercation."

Angus leaned forward and pressed the space bar, and the video continued.

"Lord Farnley has a study at the back of his house where he keeps all the paperwork for the development. There's documents and plans and everything. It's all printed because they don't want anyone seeing it. I was looking for him one day and he'd left the study door unlocked, so I've seen it all. The estate plan is for hundreds of houses. It's practically a small town.

"Then Lord Farnley walked in on me. I pretended I hadn't looked at any of the documents, but he knew I had: they were right there in front of me. He made me promise not to say anything, and I promised, then made myself scarce."

He closed his eyes and rubbed his forehead, then faced the camera again. "I've looked up that company, Beamont Holdings, on the internet. It's run by really dodgy people. People you wouldn't want to cross. But I'm scared. They know there's going to be opposition to it, and they've been keeping it a secret. That's why I'm doing this video, as proof." He stared directly into the camera and the screen went blank.

"So how did *you* find this video?"

"My program that searches dark web websites found this."

Angus shook his head and laughed. "Bloody hell, Charlotte, do you realise how amazing you are?"

Charlotte beamed. "Don't feed my ego too much, but I am very pleased. Although this is one of the most popular video sites on the dark web, so it wasn't particularly hard to find."

"While this video isn't enough to prove Liam is innocent, it does cast doubt on his conviction," said Angus. "And it gives another possible motive for Brian's murder. It would just be circumstantial. Without any proper evidence of the plans and the others involved, there's no way they'd re-open a murder case based on that video alone."

"We need to pay Lord Farnley a visit and see if we can find and get into his study. In the meantime, Charlotte, make sure you have lots of backups of that video, and send it to Woody and Liam's lawyer."

"On it." Charlotte turned to the computer and started typing.

Chapter Thirty

Angus parked outside the main entrance of Sterling Hall. When they got out, it was eerily quiet and the large oak front door was open.

"Weird," Charlotte commented, frowning. "Last time we came, there were vehicles parked outside here and the place was locked up."

Angus walked over to the door and knocked. "Hello?" He expected the dogs to come running out, or at least the sound of them barking, but there was nothing. He knocked again: still silence.

"I think we should go in," Charlotte said. "They might not have heard us." Without waiting for a reply, she walked inside.

It took a moment for her eyes to adjust to the darkness. The hallway was large, with a stone floor partially covered by a worn rug. There were five different doorways all open.

"Hello?" Charlotte moved towards the nearest doorway and poked her head into the room. It was a lounge, full of antique furniture, with a ticking grandfather clock in the corner. She heard Angus's footsteps behind her. "No one in there," she said.

She moved to the next doorway. Beyond was a huge room: a kind of study, with an oak table in the middle that dominated the room. The table was covered with papers, documents and printouts. In the centre was an Ordnance Survey map.

Charlotte walked inside. "Do you think this is the room Brian mentioned in his video?"

Angus moved to the table and looked at the map. "Yes. The map shows the local area." He pointed to where an area was surrounded by a red line.

Charlotte took out her phone and started taking photos of the documents.

"I had a feeling you wouldn't leave Brian's death alone," said a cold, refined male voice behind them.

They both spun round.

Lord Farnley stood just inside the room, casually dressed in a pale-blue and white checked shirt and navy trousers. "You know, if you're going to start snooping around someone's house, you really should check to see whether they have CCTV or not. Why are you here?"

Angus pointed at the table. "What is all this?"

"None of your business. Better to keep your nose out."

Charlotte raised an eyebrow. "Indeed, after what happened to Brian and Darren. Maybe we should."

Lord Farnley's face darkened. "I don't know what you're talking about."

"Really? We know that Brian found this room and saw these papers, and he wanted to stop you building a new town on your land. Then he ended up murdered."

"Pure speculation. What reason would I have to kill

him? Besides, he was killed by his neighbour over an argument."

"Because he found out about your plan to build a huge new estate on your land, and the underhand way you were going about it," Angus added.

Lord Farnley huffed, and then smiled. "I suppose there's no point in denying it now. Yes, Brian found out about my plans, and opposed them, declined my generous offer to ignore what he'd seen. He was about to go blabbing to everyone, telling them. The locals are idiots: NIMBYs - Not in My Back Yards in the truest sense. They want housing, but they don't want the houses anywhere near them."

"So you will be making a tidy profit from it all being the land owner. What would you get? A percentage of the house prices sold?"

"Of course. How else would I keep this place going? It's a money pit: it costs me a bloody fortune to run."

Charlotte considered this. "Maybe you could open it up to visitors? Like Longleat, where they have a theme park in the grounds."

Lord Farnley frowned at her. "I'm not ruining this place by putting a theme park outside. My family have owned Sterling Hall for fourteen generations and despite everything that's been thrown at us, we're still here. The land for the housing is over the hill, and it would keep the estate going for decades in the future."

"Just about." Lady Farnley entered, pointing a handgun at Charlotte and Angus.

"Is that even real?" Charlotte asked, peering at the gun.

"Oh yes. Had it years: it's my father's from the war. Never mind the handgun ban in the nineties, I wasn't giving it up. And before you ask, yes, it does still work. I practise with it regularly in the barn."

"Sorry I asked," Charlotte muttered.

Angus turned back to Lord Farnley. "So you're short of money."

"Not when they they've built that, I won't be." Lord Farnley pointed to the table.

"That will take some time," said Angus. "The planning permission alone will take years, and there are bound to be objections."

Lord Farnley smirked. "The developers have people in the planning department and the council who will make sure it passes. And they've given me a generous advance payment."

"They must be making an absolute fortune, then," Angus stated.

"They will be. And a pair of two-bit private investigators like you won't stand in their way. Or in mine. It's a shame it's come to this, but you were warned."

"Warned?"

"The letters."

"You sent the letters?" Angus said.

"Yes. So what's about to happen to you is entirely your fault."

Angus laughed. "You are joking? If we're hurt in any way, the police will be on to you very quickly. Charlotte's brother is a detective chief inspector in the police. Do you think he'll let this drop?"

"I've already got away with two murders. Another two won't make any difference." Lord Farnley smirked.

"You made it look like Liam did it, but it was you who killed Darren too. What happened? Darren found out about Brian, and about the housing development?"

"He was offered a very generous package, just like Brian. But he got cold feet. Idiot."

"Look," said Angus, "if you give yourselves up now and expose the developers, the courts may be lenient."

"I'm not going to prison." Lord Farnley's face grew even redder.

"Neither am I." Lady Farnley was still cool and calm. "We can't kill them here, though. We'll have to make it look like an accident. A horrible, tragic accident."

"My brother will see straight through that," said Charlotte, scornfully.

Lord Farley raised his eyebrows. "Really? He was completely fooled by that false evidence that it was Beckett who killed Brian. He's just like all the other plods: useless."

"How dare you!" Charlotte took a step towards him, her face red. "He's a great policeman."

Lord Farnley laughed. "Oh yes, he was very good at picking up the false information I left for him. Like a golden retriever. The dog poo in the garden, killing the plants, the blood stained overall. It was all so easy."

Angus put a hand on Charlotte's shoulder. "He's baiting you, Charlotte. Don't rise to it."

Lady Farnley moved forwards. "Hand over your mobile phones."

Neither of them moved.

"I said give me your mobile phones. Now."

Angus put his phone on the table next to him, and Charlotte slowly did the same.

"Check them for other devices," Lord Farnley said.

Lady Farnley handed the gun over to her husband then went over to Charlotte and patted her down with one hand, keeping the other trained on her. "Aha!" she exclaimed, when she got to her ankle. "What have we here? Another mobile? Naughty naughty." She took the phone and put it on the table.

Lady Farnley turned to Angus and with a smile, patted him down too. "Nothing on him. What are we going to do with them.

Lord Farnley pointed to a door behind them. "Put them in there while we decide." He pointed to the door behind them. "Open that door, and go inside."

Chapter Thirty-One

Angus and Charlotte found themselves inside a small room. It was the same width as the study they'd just come from, but not as long. It was filled with cardboard boxes of papers and old office furniture, a musty smell hung in the air. There was a small frosted-glass window high up on the wall, but not even a toddler could have got through it.

The door closed behind them and the lock clicked.

"Shit, they've locked us in." Charlotte went to the door and tried it anyway. "Oh God, I hate enclosed spaces. This is not going to end well." She turned to Angus. "Are they going to kill us?"

"I suspect that's what they're planning, yes," said Angus. "Now is the time to tell me that you have a third hidden mobile phone."

Charlotte spread her hands. "I haven't. Note to self, carry an extra extra mobile phone, preferably somewhere discreet. Not that there's going to be a next time." She wandered around the room looking at the walls, then at the tiny window. "I really, really hate enclosed spaces.

How long do you think it will be before they come back?"

Angus went over to Charlotte and put his hands on her shoulders. "Try not to panic, Charlotte. Think of your happy place."

"I can't: this room is too small. My happy place is a beach in the Seychelles."

"Close your eyes and think of that, then."

She closed her eyes for about ten seconds, then opened them again. "Nope. It's not happening."

"We need to find a way out of here."

"No shit, Sherlock," Charlotte snapped.

Angus took a deep breath. "We need to find a way out of here *quickly*." He went over to the door and tried it too. It didn't budge, and shoulder-barging it wouldn't help as it opened into the study. "Charlotte, start searching the boxes for anything that might help us."

Charlotte started opening the cardboard boxes. "This one is just documents." Angus joined her and they spent a few minutes opening boxes and looking through them. In the corner was an old table, again covered in boxes, and Angus began moving some of them.

"Stop!" cried Charlotte.

Angus looked up. "What?"

"There, on the table, next to you."

Angus turned and saw a telephone. He picked it up and examined it. It had no dial, just three buttons labelled *Study, Lounge, Bedroom*. "It isn't connected to anything..." He held up the bare wire at the end.

Charlotte came over and took it from him. "It's an old intercom phone, for use inside the house."

Angus turned away and delved into a nearby box.

Charlotte carried on looking at the phone, then scanned

157

the room. "If I rewire it, I should be able to connect it to the phone system. The junction box is over there." She pointed to the corner of the room, where there was a large box with multiple wires leading into it.

Angus smiled. "Connect it to the landline? That's a bit old school for you, isn't it?"

"No, actually. I went on a course about five years ago where we spent a couple of hours phreaking."

Angus's brow furrowed. "Phreaking?"

"The instructor was a man in his sixties who'd trained as an engineer well before computer science degrees existed. Clive, that was his name...Anyway, he took us through phreaking, playing around with old telecoms equipment. He had loads of it, all bought from eBay or collected from the tip."

"And?"

"It's old school, but plenty of people still have old equipment, especially in houses like this. Third-world countries have older systems, too. It's a very important part of cybersecurity training to know about older phone systems. Before the internet spread outside the government and universities, people used to practise phreaking to get free long-distance phone calls. You know, in the days before Skype or Zoom. Remember?"

"Just about. How did we ever survive without the internet? I've never even heard of phreaking." Angus's eyes shifted to the unit on the wall.

"Most people haven't," said Charlotte. "Hopefully, my training will pay off."

"OK, so what do you need me to do?"

"Pull the cover off the phone unit up there: I need to see what's under it. I don't think I can reach, but you will."

Angus took a chair, stood on it and lifted the plastic

cover off. It was caked in dust. He got down, placed it on the floor and brushed the dust off his hands.

Charlotte stood on the chair and scrutinised the unit. "I'm not sure this will work, but I'll give it my best shot. I'm pretty sure that if I can connect the intercom to the black wire on the left, it will let me dial out. I need a screwdriver, if possible, or a knife."

Angus resumed looking through the boxes. Charlotte stepped off the chair, put the intercom on another box and started to examine it. "Luckily, this was made in the days when things were built well. I'm not sure how old it is, but it's at least from the sixties. Maybe the seventies."

Charlotte picked up the intercom carefully and turned it in her hands, then looked at the bottom. "I need to get these screws out. Any luck?" She watched Angus sort through another box.

"Not yet. It's all junk: old pots and pans, photos, that sort of thing." He delved into another box, lifting out some old books. "Aha!" He pulled out a table knife. "Any good?"

Charlotte held out her hand for it. "Possibly. Let's see..." The knife slipped a little, but she increased the pressure and the screw started to loosen. One by one, she removed the screws and lifted off the plastic cover.

Inside was a circuit board. "Wow, it's like new." Charlotte held it up and took a closer look, then pointed to a large metal section in the middle. "That's the tone generator circuit. Normally, it would be used to connect to one of the other phones on the intercom. I'm going to connect it to that junction box and dial 999."

Angus pushed his glasses up his nose. "How long will that take?"

"Not long. I just need to remember how to get it to dial a number." She looked at the unit again. "Ah yes, I remember now. See this bit of the circuit? That's the modulator. It makes the pulse sound that dials out. Once I've connected it to the box up there, it will think this is a real telephone."

Charlotte stood on the chair, pulled out one of the wires and disconnected it from the box, then plugged in the intercom. A landline dial tone sounded from the intercom speaker. She grinned. "Bingo!" The wire didn't stretch far, so she had to hold the unit up. "I need you to hold the box while I dial out."

Angus put another chair next to Charlotte's and stood on it.

"OK... Let's try." She touched the modulator unit with the knife and a tone sounded. She did it twice more.

The landline dial tone came back.

Charlotte grimaced. "I can't remember what the tone for nine is. I guess that was one."

"Try a different one."

She did it again, this time she turned the modulator a little more. The tone was different, but again nothing followed.

She took a deep breath. "I just need to be patient: that's what Clive would do. OK, again, adjusting the modulator slightly more."

This time the touch-tone sounded longer and deeper. They heard the sound of ringing.

"Hello, emergency. Which service, please?"

"Police," Charlotte and Angus said in unison.

"Putting you through."

"Police emergency, state the problem, please?"

"Hello?" said Charlotte. "Oh thank God! We need help: we're being held captive by Lord and Lady Farnley near Okehampton, Devon. Sterling Hall. We think they're going to kill us. Please come quickly."

There was a moment of silence on the other end of the line. "You're being held captive? What's your name, madam?"

"Charlotte Lockwood. My brother is DCI Mark Lockwood of Devon and Cornwall Police."

"Can you tell me your exact location?"

"We're in a hidden room in their mansion, Sterling Hall" Charlotte explained, then looked at Angus. "God, it sounds completely ridiculous, doesn't it?"

"Who is there with you, madam?"

"Angus Darrow. He's my partner."

"Tell them Lady Farnley has a gun," said Angus.

"They have a gun. Look, can you put me through to my brother? DCI Lockwood."

"Hold on a moment, madam."

The line fell silent. "Hello? Hello?" said Charlotte.

Angus put his palm on his forehead. "Charlotte, as much as you want to speak to Mark, please just let the police call handler tell everyone about the emergency. That way, they can get to us more quickly. You can talk to Mark when we're out of here."

Charlotte bit her lip. "I didn't think of that."

After what seemed like a very long time, the call handler came back on. "Putting you through, madam."

"Charlie?"

"Mark, we're at Sterling Hall. Lord and Lady Farnley killed Brian and they've locked us in a room. They're going to kill us. You have to come now."

"Is this some sort of joke? If so, it's not a very good one."

"I'm not joking! You have to come quickly. They're going to kill us and you need to stop them. They have guns."

"All right, hold tight. I'm in Exeter, but I'll get the firearms team on the case. Angus, are you there?"

"I am."

"If you let anything happen to my little sister, I'll kill you. That's if they don't get to you first."

The line went dead. Charlotte disconnected the intercom and they stepped off the chairs.

"Well done." Angus put the intercom on a box and hugged Charlotte.

She hugged him back. "Well done Clive, really. I'm going to contact him when we're out of this and thank him."

Angus chuckled and reluctantly let go of her, "I'll go with you. Now we need to wait for Woody. I give it twenty minutes."

"What happens if they come in here before the police arrive?"

Angus grasped her shoulders firmly. "They won't lay a finger on us. I promise," he said.

Their faces hovered close together, proximity creating a sudden intimacy. For a heartbeat, Charlotte lost herself, oblivious to their dangerous situation.

Her gaze met Angus's. A silent communication passed between them, they were inches apart.

Then, Charlotte's smart watch buzzed on her wrist.

Reality jolted back into place, breaking their moment of connection.

Charlotte looked at her watch. "The Farnley's must have taken my phone somewhere, that was an alert that my phone isn't close by anymore."

Every minute that passed seemed like an hour. Angus went back to one of the boxes and found an old metal lamp, without a bulb or shade. It was heavy and might be a useful weapon when they opened the door. *If* they opened the door.

Charlotte paced, sat down, looked at her watch and paced some more.

Twenty minutes passed.

"Shouldn't they be here by now?" Charlotte clenched her fists.

"Give them time."

"Wouldn't they send a team from Okehampton police station?"

"Not when there's guns."

"I can't believe she kept an illegal handgun."

"There are plenty around still—"

They were interrupted by a knock at the door. Charlotte jumped, and Angus took his place behind the door, the lamp raised above his head.

The lock clicked and the door opened. "Charlotte? Angus?"

Angus exhaled and lowered the lamp.

The door opened fully and Woody came in with an armed police team behind him.

Charlotte flung herself at Woody. "Thank God. Have you got them?"

"Not yet. A team are searching the grounds and house for them."

"Lady Farnley has a vintage handgun. I don't know about Lord Farnley."

"Good job I brought the armed team with me, then." Woody turned to Angus and saw the lamp he was still holding. "You planning on using that, or are you taking it home as a souvenir?"

Angus put it down. "Sorry. Just making sure I was armed with something."

"I need to get out of this room," Charlotte said, and hurried into the study. The others followed her out.

She took a few deep breaths, turning to take in the space. "That's better. I don't think I could have handled it much longer in there."

"Since when have you not liked enclosed spaces?" Woody asked incredulous.

"I've never liked them. I nearly passed out when I visited Exeter's Underground Passages."

Woody turned to Angus. "Was she like this the whole time?"

"She was too busy getting us out of there to panic too much."

Woody grinned. "Mate, you deserve a medal for putting up with her in a confined space."

"Shut up, Mark." Charlotte folded her arms and glared at him.

"What's all this about planning permission, then?" Woody asked.

Angus pointed to the table. "It's all on there. Lord and Lady Farnley have been secretly working with a company, to put out plans for a new town, or at least so many houses that it seems like it."

Woody rolled his eyes. "Let me guess – for wodges of cash."

"Yep."

"They admitted killing Brian and Darren." Charlotte said.

"Did they?" Woody took a deep breath. "Well, if that's true, then it looks like your man Liam will be let off."

"That'll take time though, won't it?" Charlotte asked.

"It could. But we need proof that they did it."

"I have it," said Charlotte. "Not only did they admit to

it, but I found a video Brian made the night he was killed. I'll show it to you."

"Wow," said Woody. "Maybe you should join the police as a detective, Charlie."

Charlotte grinned. "Not a chance."

They heard scuffling in the hallway. Moments later, Lord and Lady Farnley were pushed in the room by officers, cuffs held their arms behind their backs.

An officer turned to Woody. "They tried to make a run for it, sir, but they only got as far as the stable block. Found them hiding in the hay bales."

"This is a disgrace!" Lord Farnley exclaimed in a disgusted tone.

"You pointed a gun at us and held us hostage!" Charlotte cried. "You were going to kill us!"Lady Farnley's eyes narrowed and she gave Charlotte a contemptuous look.

"Take them away," Woody commanded. "I'll follow shortly."

The pair were led out. "Who's going to look after my dogs?" wailed Lady Farnley.

"They'll be put into kennels," an officer replied. Then the voices faded away.

Woody turned to them both. "Right, you two, you know the drill. Statements at the station, ASAP."

Angus nodded.

"I think I'll need a long lie-down in a darkened room after today," Charlotte said.

"We did it, though. We proved Liam's innocence." Angus put his arm around Charlotte's shoulder. "And you got us out of an awful situation with that intercom phone. I had no idea that was possible."

Charlotte turned, buried her face in Angus's chest and put her arms around him. They held each other for a few moments, before brisk, official sounding footsteps made them pull apart.

"They're on their way, sir," the officer said to Woody.

"Right then, see you at the station." Woody winked at Angus and left the room.

Chapter Thirty-Two

Four weeks later.

Charlotte and Angus sat on chairs in Liam's back garden. It was a gloriously sunny day.

"It's really peaceful here." Charlotte lifted her face to the sun. "I love the sound of birds chirping in the background when you sit in an English country garden."

Liam came into the garden with a tray. He was dressed in khaki shorts and a black T-shirt. "Here we are." He set down the tray and poured tea into three mugs. "I hope you don't mind mugs. Not very posh, I know. I'll let you do your own milk and sugar."

"Mugs are perfect," Angus added milk to his mug. "You get more tea."

They sat in silence for a moment before Liam spoke. "You know, I don't think I'll ever have enough words to thank you both. I thought I was going to die in that prison."

"We're just glad that justice has been done." Angus picked up a biscuit from the plate and took a bite. "Do you have any plans in the near future? A holiday, maybe?"

Liam nodded, "I had a lot of thinking time in prison. To try and cheer myself up, I used to plan things for if I ever got out. There's quite a list, but I've always wanted to walk the Camino de Santiago. I'll start with that."

"I've never heard of it," Charlotte commented.

"It's a pilgrimage walk. There are many routes, but the one I want to do is Porto to Santiago de Compostela. It starts in Porto in Portugal and finishes in Santiago de Compostela in Spain. The Cathedral is believed to have the remains of St James buried there. It's about a hundred and seventy miles, so it takes a few weeks to walk."

"That sounds like a meaningful thing to do, after everything you've been through." Angus took another biscuit.

"Yeah. It'll be a time of reflection and thanksgiving. When I was in prison, I found great solace in religion. I was an atheist, but for some reason, I rediscovered my faith. I'm going to explore that further. The pilgrimage will help, I'm sure."

Liam added milk and sugar to his own mug and sat back. "Have you seen all the news reports about the case?"

Angus shook his head. "I don't read the news much. Too depressing."

"I've seen them," Charlotte said. "The press have gone a bit nuts over it. We're mentioned, but your story of being wrongly convicted has touched the public. Lots of people have criticised the original investigation on social media."

"Did you know that your brother visited me a few days ago?" Liam asked.

Charlotte raised her eyebrows. "I didn't. What did he say?"

"He apologised for getting it wrong."

Angus and Charlotte shared a glance. "Is that all he said?"

"We didn't speak for very long, but he did seem genuinely sorry about it. I've had lawyers in touch too. No-win-no-fee offers, but part of me just wants to put it all behind me and move on. The Department of Justice have offered me £50,000 compensation. Some of the lawyers say I could get double that if I pushed it, though."

"Well, I'm sure you'll work out what you need to do, Liam," Angus said.

Liam exhaled. "I'm going to take one day at time for now, and not worry about the future. Except for planning my Camino pilgrimage."

They sat in the sun for another half hour before Charlotte and Angus left.

Back in Topsham, Charlotte perched at the breakfast bar while Angus, preparing their dinner, chopped vegetables for the stir fry.

The doorbell rang and Charlotte slipped off the stool. "I'll get that."

When she opened the door, it was Maggie from the pottery class, her eyes wild with anger. She was dressed quite smartly, in black tapered trousers and a pale-pink blouse, but her feet were planted firmly, slightly apart, as if she expected Charlotte to rush at her, and her chest heaved with emotion.

"Maggie, what are you doing here? How do you know where I live?" Charlotte frowned, then stepped outside. "Are you all right?"

"I told you to stay away," Maggie said, through gritted teeth. "But you wouldn't listen."

"Er, what do you mean?"

"He loves *me*, not you."

"What? Who?"

"I've seen you with him. Laughing and chattering, the pair of you. You've been going to his flat."

"His *flat*?" Charlotte had thought she meant Angus. Then she realised that Maggie had never met him. "You mean ... David?"

"He's mine. I told you to leave him well alone, but you didn't listen."

Suddenly, Charlotte understood. "*You* sent that letter..." The poison-pen letter she had received hadn't been from Lord Farnley, about Liam. It had been from Maggie, about David. *Oh God, she's a bunny boiler.*

"What else was I supposed to do, you stupid bitch? He's *mine*..." Maggie pulled out a large kitchen knife from behind her back and held it up, still breathing like a bull about to charge.

Charlotte stepped back into the house and slammed the door, panic coursing through her. She needed to call 999, but she also needed to check on David. Maybe Maggie had visited him first.

She went into the kitchen, where Angus was stirring a pan on the stove. "Anyone exciting?" he asked, without turning round.

"It's a madwoman with a knife."

"Ha ha, very funny."

"No, it really is! It's Maggie from my pottery class and she has a knife. She wants to kill me."

Angus turned, smiling, and saw her face. "Seriously?"

"Yes."

Angus came over to her. "Sorry, I really thought you were joking."

"I wouldn't joke about something like this."

He frowned. "But why is she threatening you?"

Charlotte didn't want to tell Angus why. She'd purposely hidden her relationship with David, if it could be called a relationship. Not because she was ashamed of David, but because deep down, she knew that David, sweet and kind as he was, wasn't Angus. "I'll explain later. I need to call the police."

Maggie's voice came through the letter box. "Come out here and face me like a woman, you bitch."

"I'll go," Angus said, and started for the door.

"No, she's got a knife!"

"I've dealt with knives before."

"You're not wearing a stab vest. I'll call the police and they can deal with her."

Charlotte ran to the study, picked up her phone and dialled 999. It was answered quickly. "Emergency, which service do you need?"

"Police."

"Putting you through."

When she got through, the situation took a short time to explain. When she hung up and went downstairs, she couldn't find Angus. He must have gone outside.

"Shit!" she cried.

Chapter Thirty-Three

Part of Angus wondered whether Charlotte had been exaggerating about having a knife-wielding pottery-class-attending woman outside her house.

But as soon as he opened the door, there she was. She was short, dumpy, and despite the knife in her hand, didn't look at all threatening.

Angus's police training took over and he stepped outside. "Hello. Are you Maggie?"

"Who are you?" she demanded. "Where's that dirty bitch?"

"I'm Angus. Why don't you put that knife down? Then you can come inside and we can all talk."

Maggie considered this idea for a moment. "No. I want to see *her*. She needs to stay away from David. I've warned her. She needs to leave him well alone."

Angus moved towards her. "Look, I understand that you're angry, but we can't talk while you've got that knife."

Maggie pointed the knife at him. "Stay away. I'm warning you!"

Angus put his hands up. "All right, but the police will

be here any minute, so it's better you put the knife down now. They don't look kindly on that sort of thing."

Maggie stood her ground. "Everything was going well until *she* came along, with her stupid blonde hair and that pathetic laugh. David loves me, not her. No one, especially not her, is getting in my way. We're meant to be together."

"Well, if you're meant to be together, then you've nothing to fear from Charlotte, have you?"

"She's been sleeping with him. She's stolen him from me."

Angus wasn't sure whether or not to believe her. Charlotte hadn't mentioned seeing anyone. Then he remembered how she'd mentioned evening commitments lately. Since she'd started the pottery class, in fact. A surge of jealousy ran through him, then he pushed it aside. He had to defuse the situation first. Then, and only then, would there be time to react. "Put the knife down," he commanded.

Maggie's hand started to shake, but she didn't lower the knife.

The front door opened and Charlotte appeared. "Angus, come inside."

Maggie turned to her. "I'm going to kill you. You took him from me," Maggie shouted. She made to go around Angus, but he blocked her and grabbed her wrist, lifting her arm up until she let go of the knife. It fell to the floor with a clang.

"Argh! Get off me!" Maggie cried.

Angus twisted her arm behind her back and held her in a tight grip.

"Let go of me!" she shouted.

Charlotte bent and picked up the knife. Only then did Angus loosen his grip and let Maggie go.

She ran towards her car, parked on the drive, but Angus

overtook her and blocked the driver door. Maggie tried to pull him away, but she was too weak.

"Give it up, Maggie," he said, folding his arms. "You're not going anywhere."

Maggie sank to the ground and began to cry.

Charlotte went into the hallway, and while keeping a lookout, took out her phone and called David. He picked up after two rings. "Hello, Charlotte."

"Hi. Strange question. Are you all right?" Charlotte asked.

"Yeah, fine. Why?"

"That's a relief. I— I'll explain next time I see you. Just wanted to check everything was OK."

"I've just closed up the cafe and shop for the night. Fancy coming over?"

Charlotte looked outside at Angus, standing his ground, and sighed. She needed to stop seeing David before things got too serious. It was Angus she wanted, and she couldn't let anything stand in her way.

"Not tonight, but tomorrow?" That would give her time to think about how she could let him down gently.

"Great, see you then."

As she ended the call, a police car pulled onto the drive.

When the police had taken their statements, Angus went into the kitchen and inspected the food he had been cooking earlier. Everything was ruined. He turned on the hot tap and started to scrape the contents of the saucepans into the bin. It wasn't quite the ending he had expected to a day like that.

Charlotte came into the kitchen and leaned against the door frame, arms folded. "I, er, I wanted to thank you for dealing with Maggie."

Angus turned off the tap and faced her. "You can't beat a bit of excitement at the end of a case." Charlotte shook her head a little.

"So you've been seeing David the pottery tutor." He picked up another saucepan and scraped more food into the bin.

"Yeah."

"And he has a mad stalker who's secretly in love with him, and she's jealous of you."

Charlotte nodded. "She's been watching him and...us."

"Well, that's certainly something to talk about next time you meet up. Did he have any idea?"

"I'm not sure. I checked he was OK, but I didn't mention Maggie. She hasn't hurt him: all her hate seems to be directed at me. I'll tell him about her tomorrow. He needs to know that she's been stalking him."

"I'm glad he's all right. Anyway, dinner is off, obviously. Shall I call for a takeaway?"

Charlotte shook her head. "I'm not hungry any more."

"You should have something, even if it's just toast. You still look pale. You're in shock." Angus came over to her, put his hands on her shoulders and looked into her eyes.

"It's not serious, you know. Me and David." It wasn't serious for her, anyway, but now that she thought about it, over the last few weeks she'd got the impression that David was taking it all a lot more seriously than her. She really needed to put the brakes on before he got hurt. She couldn't meet Angus's eyes.

Angus let go of her. "It's none of my business." He paused for a moment. "You're my friend, though, so I'll be checking he treats you right."

Charlotte smiled. "Thanks," she whispered.

Angus turned the tap on again, squirted washing-up liquid into the pans and filled them to the brim. "These need to soak for a bit." Then he moved to the dishwasher and put everything else he'd used in it. "If you're not having anything to eat, Charlotte, that's up to you. I'm starving, though, so I'm going to pick up something on the way home."

"You could order a delivery here," Charlotte said, in a small voice.

"No, I'll get going. I'll see you on Monday morning and then we can pick our next case. A few have come in recently that look interesting. Some similar ones to Liam's. They must have seen the papers."

Charlotte nodded. Then he picked up his phone and keys, and left.

Outside, Angus sat frozen in his car, stung by the news. Charlotte, was seeing someone. It didn't matter she viewed it as not serious. A wave of regret washed over him. Not only had he waited too long to admit his feelings, but he'd also unwittingly pushed her towards David with those extra pottery lessons he'd gifted her for her birthday a few weeks back. What an idiot.

He took out his phone and looked at the text he'd received from Jo, the barmaid at the Hare and Hounds, a few weeks ago.

Well done on cracking the case. If you ever fancy meeting up, let me know. Jo xxx

. . .

Angus exhaled, looked at Charlotte's house, then pressed Reply.

Hi Jo, thanks. Yes, I'd love to meet up. Let me know when you are free this week. Angus.

THE END

Pre-order the next book in the Lockwood and Darrow Series: Exe on the beach, book 6:

When a celebrity chef from Exmouth mysteriously disappears, private investigators Lockwood and Darrow are discreetly enlisted to investigate, keeping a step ahead of the relentless press. Though the chef's known mental health struggles hint at a possible explanation, as the duo delve deeper, they unearth a tangled web of secrets that suggest a far darker narrative.

The quest for truth threatens to have wide-ranging implications, placing them in the crosshairs of the town's most dangerous secrets. The pair must work swiftly to expose the truth before the town's underbelly consumes them.

My Book

Suzy Bussell

SIGN up to my newsletter on my website to get a FREE
Lockwood and Darrow short story.
www.suzybussell.com

Suzy xx

Acknowledgments

Many thanks as ever to my amazing editor Liz Hedgecock (who's also an author, check out her books on Amazon). Also, to my husband for his constant encouragement and unfailing belief in my writing.

About the Author

I started writing around 2002 starting with fan fictions. I then branched out into writing my own characters and stories, and in 2019 wrote the first Lockwood and Darrow book after Charlotte and Angus wouldn't get out of my brain unless I wrote them down. Although, as you can see, they are still there a lot of the time!

Like Charlotte, I grew up in Hertfordshire, and moved to Devon twenty years ago. It has had a profound affect on me because every book I've ever written has been set, or partly set in Devon.

I live close to the sea with my husband, three sons and two cats.

When I'm not writing, I love swimming and playing the fiddle.

Printed in Great Britain
by Amazon